THE ROYAL MARINE

DAHLIA DONOVAN

For information, contact the publisher, Hot Tree Publishing.

WWW.HOTTREEPUBLISHING.COM

EDITING & FORMATTING: HOT TREE EDITING

COVER DESIGNER: CLAIRE SMITH

ISBN-10: 1-925655-18-0

ISBN-13: 978-1-925655-18-6

10 9 8 7 6 5 4 3 2 1

DEDICATION

For the letter writers.

CHAPTER ONE

AKASH

"The fucking soldier twat broke my nose."

Akash found it almost impossible to smother the inappropriate urge to laugh loudly at the cursing man sitting on the kerb outside of the Sin Bin. "Serves you right."

"What the fuck did I do?" Scottie surged to his feet, only to be shoved back down on his arse by one of his friends, who had been hovering nearby since the evening out at the nightclub had ended in a fistfight between the manager and a patron. "Fuck."

Their evening had begun positively. Akash had, at the invitation of Rupert, BC, and Freddie, agreed to visit the new club in Cardiff. The Sin Bin had been the brainchild of retired rugby superstar Boyce "BC" Brooks and several of his former teammates: Caddock Stanford, Remi Chardin, Scott "Scottie" Monk, and Taine "Tens" Afoa. They'd pooled their money and resources to open the Sin Bin in an old warehouse on a wharf in the city.

Freddie had only just returned from his trip overseas with a non-profit organisation. The nurse had brought a friend—Hamish Ross—with him, a Royal Marine, who among other things, worked security for several non-profits. Akash had found his eyes straying to the tall blond several times through the evening.

And that, he supposed, might've been where the night took a turn for the worse.

It became painfully and awkwardly clear his friends hadn't coordinated in their efforts to find him a date. Freddie and Aled, a botanist who'd become a good friend, had brought Hamish as a potential partner for him. BC and Rupert tried to set him up with Scottie. Tempers had flared—one temper in particular.

When Scott Monk tried rather aggressively to hit on him, Akash had merely raised an eyebrow at the "call me Scottie." He found nothing about the loud, brash, and smug man attractive; a handsome face didn't make up for his appalling personality. He'd finally had to say as much to get the former rugby player turned nightclub manager to leave him alone.

His assumption that that would be the end of it had turned out to be wrong.

Wrong, wrong, so damn wrong.

When Freddie and Aled brought the thirty-nine-year-old Hamish over, the evening had perked up. He didn't mind their ten-year age gap. They'd met a few times before, but never talked in depth. They'd immediately fallen into a conversation about where in India his mother came from and how his father, then a British military officer, had met her. It seemed the blond man had travelled to some of the same places.

Things didn't kick off until after the club had closed for the evening; Scottie, predictably, hadn't taken being discounted in favour of the blond Adonis well. He made a few insulting comments Akash would rather forget about both his heritage and his job as a baker. Before anyone else could intervene, Hamish had landed a solid fist to the ranting man's jaw.

The fight started with the Royal Marine—and ended with him as well. They all waited outside for tempers to cool. Aside from the bleeding and sulking Scottie, the other former rugby players who owned the Sin Bin had immediately apologised to Akash.

"Say you're sorry." Taine grabbed Scottie by the collar to yank him up to his feet and drag him in front of Akash. "Well? Go on. If you want to stay a partner and the manager of *our* club, you will learn to get a sodding grip on your temper. Got it?"

Scottie elbowed the massive Scottish-Maori man in the side. "Get the fuck off me."

Akash couldn't help lifting his eyebrow at the man for the second time that evening. He'd known blustering bullies like Scottie his entire life—and never allowed himself to be intimidated by them. "Something you'd like to say? Or can I get on with my evening?"

Snorts of amusement echoed all around them, which only served to anger Scottie further. He clenched his fist and took another menacing step forward. Akash merely ran his fingers through his slightly shaggy black hair. His indifference apparently threw the larger man.

"Right. So, I'm fucking sorry for whatever, but you're still attractive." Scottie paused midstep, still clutching at his nose. "Wanna grab a pint with me?"

"Have you been concussed one too many times?" Akash leant in closer to make a show of peering carefully at Scottie. "The only way I'd share a pint with you would be if I bashed you upside the head with it."

"Tetchy, tetchy, tetchy." BC reached his long arm between them and pressed Scottie backwards. "Think maybe we should call it a night, yeah?"

Akash glanced over his shoulder to see Hamish in a whispered conversation with Wyatt, his American friend and Aled's husband. He turned back to where BC had slipped an arm around Scottie to hold him up. "Might want to get some coffee in him," he suggested.

"Might take more than a coffee." BC winked at him before dragging Scottie toward the parking area. "Ginger Spice'll call you in the morning."

Akash grinned at BC's nickname for Graham. He envied the two men, who seemed to have such fun with their life together. His thoughts drifted, and it took a moment to realise everyone had gone, leaving him alone with Hamish. "Right."

"Can I give you a lift?" Hamish sounded as if he had no intention of taking no for an answer; he gave Akash hopeful smile. "I promise to get you home safely."

"I've no doubt." Akash shook his head, and laughed at the man. "Fine. I'd rather not try to find an Uber or something at this hour, and I have to be at the bakery early in the morning."

On the whole, Akash usually handled silence relatively well. Working alone in his bakery, it never oppressed him as it did others, which made his inability to remain quiet while trapped in Hamish's vehicle all the more surprising. *Shut up. Shut up. SHUT. UP. God, I'm humiliating myself.*

Blathering about the finer points of the spices he often used in his cooking didn't exactly scream sexual seduction. The man driving brought out the chattering numpty in him— one he'd never known existed. He didn't like it.

Hamish chuckled after several minutes, breaking Akash out of his thoughts. "Breathing would probably be a good thing."

Akash covered his face with his hand and spoke with an embarrassed burble of laughter, "Yes, it just might."

"You're charming." Hamish reached over to catch Akash by the wrist and drag his hand away from his face. "Completely charming."

Akash directed Hamish toward the building that housed not only his bakery but his flat as well. "Thanks for the lift." He glanced at the man out of the corner of his eye. "Fancy having supper with me some time?"

Did I just—I did. Bloody hell, I did.

Hamish's midnight blue eyes searched his briefly before he reached out with calloused and scarred fingers to catch Akash's jaw. "May I?"

"You could always try and find out." Akash almost laughed in surprise when his own voice came out as steady as always. Those hard fingers rubbed against the scruff on his jaw, sending pleasurable waves along his skin. "Do you always need an invitation for a kiss?"

"Only the first one." Hamish smiled wolfishly. His grin revealed identical dimples in his cheeks, though Akash lost sight when the man leant forward until their lips connected, awkwardly at first. Their kiss became heated quickly until they both pulled away, mouths open and breaths coming in quick gasps. He could hear Hamish swallowing a few times before he cleared his throat. "Sleep well."

Smug. Attractive. Bastard.

They exchanged numbers before Akash clambered out of the black Mercedes SUV. To his surprise he did manage to sleep well, dreaming of a sexy blond military man. It took the persistent nudging of his cat to drag him into waking up.

Hangover? Check. Ganesh sitting on my head? Check. Bakery to open? Check. Incredibly attractive men fighting over me? Daft.

Sitting up slowly in bed, Akash shoved his long-haired golden kitten off his head. Ganesh had been a gift from his younger sister, Shanti, and his elder sister, Padma. His parents hadn't liked the idea of their only son moving out on his own.

Akash covered his face with his pillow, breathing out deeply into the cool silk covering it. He didn't even need to look at the alarm clock to know he'd slept in far too long. He should've been elbow deep in dough an hour ago; if he rushed, they might open on time.

Damn it.

Akash winced at the shrill ring of his mobile phone. *Maybe I should hire a morning manager.* He ignored the phone for the moment and tried to get his brain in gear.

In Cornwall, Akash hadn't been trapped in the bakery. He found it ironic that he'd moved to Cardiff in part to improve his social life only to find almost no time for it with all the extra work. Eventually he'd bring in more help to allow him to actually take time off instead of being up before dawn and crawling into bed when the day was done.

Ganesh leapt from the pillow onto his stomach and finally onto the floor. *Insane creature.* His phone gave a cheerful beep, and he grabbed it off the nightstand to silence it. A quick glance showed a text from Graham.

Graham: How the hell did you wind up on two blind dates with equally attractive men? After a complete desert of dating since that last bloke, the one who brought your supplies, who you dumped after a month.

Akash: Good karma. Not exactly blind since I'd met them both before. And he dumped me.

Graham: Knobhead.

Graham: He was the knobhead, if you were wondering. We stayed in Cardiff last night with Tens. Your bakery open yet? We're all half-starved.

Akash: Haven't quite made it downstairs yet.

Graham: Lazy pillock. Get your arse up.

Akash: Bring coffee, and I'll think about making some of those fruit and cheese pastries you like. I might even tell you about kissing Hamish.

Graham: You kissed? Be there in five.

Akash forced himself to get out of bed and into the shower. He got a whiff of his own breath. "Bloody hell. I smell like death warmed over and baked in a quiche."

Attractive.

Right. Shower. Clothes. Baking.

No wanking in the shower.

Why am I still thinking about that kiss?

Maybe a bit of wanking in the shower.

CHAPTER TWO

HAMISH

"Morning, sunshine."

Hamish lifted his head from his desk to pin Lily with a glare. He'd woken up at the office after his night out and gone for a run before returning just in time for her to intrude on his morning. "Have I threatened to fire you yet this week?"

"Did someone miss their morning wank?" Lily placed one of the two coffee cups she held in front of him before dropping into the chair across from his own. "Did you sleep here?"

Hamish dragged his fingers through his slightly greasy blond hair. He desperately needed a shower and a few paracetamol—and a nap wouldn't hurt. The coffee would have to do him for now. "Vinnie texted me on my way home to come by the office after I left the club last night; I might've brought a few pints to have with him."

"That explains why I found him underneath his desk snoring like a busted engine and cuddled up to an empty bottle." Lily propped her feet up on his desk. "I thought you two stopped overindulging after that time in London when you were in your twenties."

"Lils." Hamish had tried to block out the memory of getting so wasted that their clothes, wallets, and even socks had been nicked off them. Lily had rescued both of them before their commanding officer had found out. "What happened to being sworn to secrecy? Hadn't we decided to chalk that up to youthful enthusiasm and stupidity?"

"Stupidity being the keyword. Okay, okay." She sipped her coffee, her green eyes alight with pure amusement. "So, Earp tells me you met someone last night."

Hamish made a mental note to kill his business partner. Wyatt "Earp" Hardy was a former Navy SEAL who co-owned Hardy & Ross: Security & Protection, better known as HRSP with him. They offered risk assessments for businesses and individuals, along with security for non-profits. It had made their transition from active duty military to civilian life easier to handle.

"Hamster?"

He blinked at Lily as she snapped her fingers at him. "What?"

"Meeting someone? Last night? Bar fights? How much did you drink last night?" She smirked at him over the edge of her coffee cup. "I can't believe I missed all the excitement."

"If I give you a raise will you go away?"

Lily saluted him with her coffee. "Did you kiss him?"

"No comment."

"That's a yes."

Hamish reached an arm out to knock her boots off his desk. "Why don't you go yell at Vinnie? I'm sure he'll appreciate it."

Watching her leave, Hamish had to chuckle when he heard loud arguing several minutes later. Lily Wilson and Vincent Smith had grown up across the street from one another. He'd met them on their first day of military service. The trio had been fast friends ever since.

When Hamish made the decision to retire, Lily and Vinnie hadn't been far behind. Their loyalty had touched him. He'd also called them blooming morons for throwing away their careers.

Slightly more than six years later, Hamish believed they'd all made a wise decision. The company had flourished; their expertise had been in high demand. Pride filled him, knowing they'd built it together out of nothing.

Wyatt had brought his own group with him, three men who had served with him as Navy SEALs: Trace "Breach" Tifft, Cole "Voodoo" Willis, and Adam "Scorch" Wallach. American soldiers loved their nicknames. *Not that we're any better.*

"Oi, Hamster, go shower," Lily yelled while walking by his office door. "Like, now, before you stench up the entire room."

Hamish gave a sniff to his underarm and immediately regretted it. "Bloody hell, I smell like Vinnie's socks."

Thanking all the saints that they'd had the foresight to build showers in the loo facilities of their office, Hamish grabbed the bag of clothes he kept in his locker. Maybe his headache would fade after he drowned himself under hot water for an hour.

When Hamish had started searching for the perfect place for their office, he'd stumbled on a fantastic deal for a warehouse in one of the old wharfs in Cardiff. They'd put more money into renovations than they had in purchasing the building. The upgrades had more than paid for themselves in allowing them to function better.

Thirty minutes in the shower cleared away the remnants of his hangover. Hamish could still taste Akash on his lips, even after a rather vigorous brushing of his teeth. He couldn't shake the ghost of their kiss from his memory.

"Hey, Hamster, word around the office is you met someone last night. What's it been? Twenty years since your last date? Did you remember how it works?" Nye leant against one of the rows of lockers while Hamish finished dressing. "Need a tutorial? Bet I could find you one online."

Rolling his eyes, Hamish chose to ignore the idiot and continued lacing up his trainers. Nye had been the last to join their Marine unit, and the first to leave it after losing both his left arm and leg in an explosion. He'd been one of the first people to join the company when they started it; he'd grown tired of, in his own words, "sitting at home on my arse doing sod all."

"Well?" Nye used his prosthetic leg to block Hamish's escape route.

Hamish folded his arms across his chest with his jaw set stubbornly. He had no intentions of nattering on about his brief moment with Akash. "Go bother Lils."

"And lose another limb? Not a sodding chance." Nye grinned at him—disgusting morning person that he was. "If you see Akash again, tell him his sister owes me a date."

"How the—"

"His little sister volunteers with the same group I do once a month. She's a sweetheart. Shanti's her name. Beautiful girl." Nye kicked his foot against the floor. "On second thought, maybe don't tell her only brother I'm dating his youngest sibling."

Hamish grabbed a towel to rub through his still dripping hair. "Nye? Go away."

Nye gave another grin. "Why don't you stop by his bakery this morning? Our noon meeting isn't going to happen, since it's already eleven and none of us is awake enough for it. Go grab us something to nosh on—and maybe kiss the baker."

"*Nye.*"

"I'm going, I'm going." Nye paused on his way out the door. "I'll tell the others the meeting will start late since you're getting food."

Hamish balled up the damp towel and flung it in the laughing idiot's direction. "Tosser."

Hamish put on a rumpled T-shirt from his bag, then ripped it off immediately and tossed it back inside. He'd grab one of the dress shirts hanging up in his office instead. None of them had eaten breakfast; pastries would be delicious. Might as well make a good impression if he had to go out.

I am hungry.

It's not too obvious if I show up the morning after, is it?

A memory of dark eyes sparkling in the dim interior lighting of the vehicle flashed into his mind. Hamish glanced up at his own reflection in the mirror. He had to admit to himself that Akash had definitely caught his attention.

Correction.

I'm fucking starving.

"Oi. Hamish?"

Hamish paused in the middle of changing his shirt. "Yeah?"

"Emergency call from that one client."

Shit.

It's always something. Akash'll have to wait.

CHAPTER THREE

AKASH

By noon, Akash found himself elbow deep in rough puff pastry, covered in flour, and studiously avoiding calls from Freddie, Jack, and Aled. They'd all likely heard gossip from Graham, who'd stopped by earlier. His three closest friends would want details on his brief moment with the dishy Royal Marine, but he didn't necessarily care to divulge any of his secrets yet.

Not without a few glasses of wine.

His old barber friend Jack Sasaki predictably seemed far more interested in Scottie than Hamish. The half-Japanese, half-Cornish man had a serious fetish for rugby—both the game and the players. Akash told him not to bother. The hot-tempered bar manager shouldn't be dating anyone, not with his anger issues.

Not me, at least.

Of the three Robinson children, Akash boasted the calmest and most balanced temperament. His elder sister took after their mother—strong and intensely forceful at times, but she also tended to separate herself from them for long periods. Shanti, the baby of the family, had an independent streak that could stretch across the globe.

Up until recently, Akash had lived in Fowey with his family, running the bakery with his mum and dad, while his elder sister pursued a career as a paediatrician, and his younger sibling studied fashion design. After a lot of serious thought last year, he'd made the decision to open a second bakery in Cardiff. His family loved him unconditionally, and he loved them, but they could be fairly stifling at times.

Plus the hints.

So many sodding hints about dating.

The elephant in the room as far as his parents went had to be their belief that he'd gotten serious in a relationship. They didn't understand why he couldn't settle down and have children. He'd fled to avoid dealing with it, even though Shanti insisted they wouldn't care.

After all, he'd never brought a date home once. They knew he'd dated. He assumed they thought his "boyfriends" were girlfriends.

One step at a time, Akash, right?

Show them I can live on my own before I explain I'd rather be buggered by a man than marry a woman.

"Akash?"

He glanced up from the Bombay potatoes that he'd been cooking up to go in his Indian-spiced pasties, to find Shanti poking her head into the kitchen. "Shouldn't you be in class?"

"Lunch." Shanti danced around the room, all energy and flowing skirts. She hopped up onto one of the few clean counters. "Mummy wants to know if you're coming home this coming weekend."

"Why?" Akash grimaced, realising his memory had failed him once again. "What did I forget this time?"

"Their wedding anniversary?"

"Bollocks." He ran his hands through his hair. "Stop giggling at me."

"You've got so much flour in your hair that you look like Papa." She reached over to grab a folded towel to toss to him. "How did your blind dates go?"

Akash narrowed his eyes on his little sister suspiciously. "Who've you been talking to, Shanti?"

Shanti waved a slender hand toward the tray of cooling pasties. "I'll sing for my supper."

Rolling his eyes at her, Akash grabbed a plate to dish one up for her. He put the rest into a basket to go out front. One of his two employees would likely be in shortly to pick them up for him.

With his parents handling the bakery in Fowey, Akash had been forced to hire additional help to run the front of the bakery. He preferred to be in the back creating all of his Hindi-Cornish fusion delicacies. When a pair of twins came looking for work, he'd hired them on the spot; Alice worked in the early mornings with him, while Alex helped in the afternoons.

The nineteen-year-olds were generally sweet and cheerful youngsters who'd taken the job to support themselves. They occasionally came in together. It depended on their university schedules.

When Alex had come in one afternoon with a busted lip, Akash forced him into the kitchen and cleaned him up. The story of their not-so-pleasant stepfather came tumbling out of the young man. With the help of several of his friends, they managed to get the twins into their own place not far from the bakery.

Now they seemed to adore him. They often arrived for work early and left late. Akash insisted they take their university courses seriously, allowing them to study on their breaks; Shanti teasingly referred to them as his children—his teenage, blond bombshell twins.

"Well?" Akash returned his attention to his sister, who grinned innocently at him before nibbling at the pasty. "Who told you about the accidental double blind date?"

"Nye."

"Who?" He thought the name sounded vaguely familiar, but his memory had always been awful. "Is that one of your school friends?"

"Not exactly." Shanti took an overly large bite and made a show of chewing as slowly as possible.

Must be a boy.

"What's this Nye like then? Did you meet him at university?" Akash gave her a knowing glance before starting to clean up the kitchen. He had another batch of pasties to make—this time curry-flavoured ones. "Does he treat you well?"

"Bloody mind reader." Shanti flicked a small piece of potato at him. "He works with Hamish, which is how I know about your being double-booked for a blind date last night. Wyatt apparently told him all about it."

"He works with…." Akash trailed off, trying to remember what Hamish had mentioned about his former marine mates. *Nye?* "Is he the one who lost an arm and a leg?"

Shanti smiled at him—a genuinely brilliant expression that he couldn't recall seeing on her face before. "He's great, Aki. I adore him. He's sweet and strong and wonderful. You'll love him."

Aki?

His conniving little sister usually only trotted out his old childhood nickname if she wanted him to do something. Akash let her stew in her thoughts while he carefully stacked the dishwasher. He wiped down the surface and finally turned to find her tapping her fingers against the counter impatiently.

"Aki?"

"Shanti." Akash leant back against the table and folded his arms across his chest. "What am I doing now?"

"Bring Hamish to family dinner this weekend?" She brought her hands up in supplication. "Please?"

"Why? So they'll be happier with your choice?" He had a sudden flash of insight. Their parents wouldn't mind Shanti dating an older man—his disability shouldn't matter to them either. "You're not preggers, are you?"

"What? No." She threw another towel at his head. "He wants to get married."

"*Married?*" Akash dropped the cloth in his hand. He blinked at her several times, trying to process what he'd heard. "Married? How long have you known each other? You haven't been in Cardiff that long."

"A few months."

"Well, no wonder you want me to be the story Mummy and Papa focus on." Akash shook his head and dragged his fingers through his hair. "Why am I even considering it?"

"Because you're the best brother in the world?" Shanti flew off the counter and into his arms. "Thank you. *Thank you.* Why are you so worried? Mummy and Papa know you're gay. They don't mind, Aki."

"You don't *know* for sure that they're aware of my dating preferences." Akash had never told them; he'd been too afraid of their disappointment. "You're assuming."

"Aki." She frowned at him with concern evident on her face. "Seriously? It's the worst kept secret in the family. We all know. I figured you moved to Cardiff to date, yet you never go anywhere outside of the bakery. It's a big city with no parents staring over your shoulder. Why haven't you dated more?"

Deciding not to delve into his dismal attempts to date in Cardiff or the fact that he worked more now than he ever had, Akash tried to ignore his sister, knowing it was never a good idea. She ranted on for a good five minutes. He flicked flour at her periodically, which she merely glared at.

"Just leave it. I said we'd go. I'm taking your word that our parents won't banish me." Akash held a hand up to stop her from continuing. "If this blows up in our faces, I'm blaming you."

"It won't." She smiled brightly at him, dancing around in a

tight circle. "They'll love Nye—and Hamish. Promise."

Bollocks.

Easy for her to say.

In his heart, Akash knew his parents loved him unconditionally. He did. Coming out to them had just always seemed like a mountain far too massive to climb; he suspected fighting through his unfounded fears might actually be the hardest part.

CHAPTER FOUR

HAMISH

The days after the encounter at the Sin Bin dragged by excruciatingly slowly. Hamish had never made it over to the bakery, and now he found his mind constantly straying to thoughts of a certain brown-eyed baker. It took immense willpower to concentrate on his speaking engagements and the paperwork that came with being responsible for the business.

Aside from security/risk assessments and protection details, HRSP offered speaking engagements to corporations, universities, and the military. They'd built up quite a reputation and client list over the years. It should've provided a sufficient distraction.

It didn't.

"Hamster." Wyatt barged into his office and sank onto

one of the chairs across from his desk. "Why the hell are you doing paperwork? You hate it. Have you called him yet? Aled's dying to know."

"Aled's dying to know?" Hamish didn't buy that excuse for a moment. "You're a gossiping twat."

"That's a no, then. What's the matter with you? He's hot—he can fucking cook. Have you tried those pie things he bakes? You're not going all weirdly stuffy and British again, are you?" Wyatt, in his typical sharp-eyed manner, found the tender spots in Hamish's armour and needled him ruthlessly. "Dude. Text him. Send a fucking pigeon. Scottie has zero chance with him, but he's not the only man in Cardiff."

Hamish involuntarily crushed the invoice in his hand, the one he'd been pretending to peruse when the American twat interrupted him. "Bloody Yank."

"Oh, I'm sorry. Did I hit the mark?" Wyatt chuckled. "It's almost lunch. Go pick something up at his bakery. I know that *you know* where it's at."

"*Earp.*" Hamish tried to silence his old friend with a glare, but Wyatt only hummed under his breath and ignored him. "Don't you have a desk of your own? Aren't you supposed to be working on the report for that new client?"

Wyatt's grin only widened until he resembled a shark scenting blood in the water. "Text him, Hamster. Don't fuck up because of the massive stick up your ass."

"Go. Away."

Once Wyatt retreated to his own office, still chuckling loudly, Hamish tapped his fingers restlessly against the desk. The obnoxious twit had a point. *Several, actually. I won't tell him though, his ego's massive enough.* He shoved the papers away from him; invoices could wait.

I am a bit peckish.

And Akash's bakery is only a ten-minute drive.

"Hammy Hamster." Lily slid on her socked feet out of her office to block his path. "Grab us some pasties, will you? Nye wants the curry potato ones."

He tried to step around her, but she danced around. "*Lils.*"

"Might want to spruce yourself up a bit." She laughed when he grabbed her by the shoulders to move her out of the way. "Comb your hair at least."

"And brush your teeth," Vinnie shouted from his office.

"Shine your shoes?" Nye offered.

"Thanks ever so much." Hamish pinched the bridge of his nose while everyone in the office yelled out their suggestions. "I hate each and every one of you both individually and collectively."

Arses.

The short drive provided only a slim opportunity for Hamish to collect his thoughts. *Don't get ahead of yourself. You're asking him out on a date.* Akash might've changed his mind.

Parking outside the bakery, Hamish breathed out deeply before hopping out of his vehicle and striding purposefully inside. Two blond teenagers who looked so much alike that they could only be siblings smiled at him from behind the counter. The brother's hand shot out to offer him a sample.

"Can I help you?" the girl asked. "Want a tart?"

Her brother pulled on her arm. "Not sure he's here for us."

Hamish narrowed his eyes. "Is Akash in?"

"Are you the one he told us about? I'm Alice. That's Alex." She lifted up the partition to let him behind the counter, and practically shoved him through the door into the kitchen area. "Akash. You've got a visitor."

CHAPTER FIVE

AKASH

Curry pasties? Done.

Coconut tarts? Done.

Curry lamb and potato pies? Done.

Sweet saffron scones? In the oven.

Me? Elbow deep in flour, caster sugar, and coconut milk.

A shout from Alice pulled his attention from the dough for candied ginger scones in his hands. The twins generally handled customers well, so it didn't seem likely they'd encountered a problem. Akash could only stare stupidly when the door swung open and a broad-shouldered blond suddenly filled the doorway.

Hamish.

In the few days since visiting the Sin Bin, Akash hadn't been able to get the man and his kiss out of his mind. He'd contemplated calling, but hadn't yet managed to pluck up the courage. Hamish strolling casually into his bakery hadn't even occurred to him.

"Are you hungry? I've got fresh scones." Akash wiped his dirty hands on the blue striped apron tied around his waist.

Hamish jolted forward as if shoved, glancing over his shoulder to glare at the giggling teenagers.

"Don't mind the twins," Akash said. "They're harmless."
Mostly harmless.

"A fairly impressive shove for two slight kids who barely come up to my shoulder." Hamish stepped further into the kitchen, allowing Akash to see the two faces fighting to get a view through the round window in the door. "What exactly are they expecting me to do?"

Akash rolled up a small piece of dough into a ball and with a steady aim launched it at the window, chuckling when the twins squeaked and fell away from the door. He dusted his hands off yet again and strove for calm in the overwhelming presence of the man in front of him. "Scone? Pasty? Pie? Are you hungry?"

Hamish made his way around the long work tables, stopping just before he bumped into Akash. "*Am* I hungry?"

Akash blinked up at him. "Well, you'd know, wouldn't you? I'm a baker—not a psychic."

Hamish caught Akash by the front of his apron and dragged him closer. He captured Akash's lips with his own for a crushing kiss, leaving both of them shuddering for breath. "*Shit.* You muck with my control."

"Me?" Akash tugged his apron free and stumbled backwards. His lips felt swollen from just one kiss. "You're the one who barged into my kitchen."

"I was shoved."

"You *barged* into my kitchen while I'm making tarts." Akash ignored his protest.

Hamish bent forward to peer down at the pastries. "They look more like scones."

"I meant scones. Don't be an arse." Akash glanced over to find their audience of two had returned. "You two get back to work."

"Aled mentioned you worked with your family." Hamish appeared to be trying to lower the sexual tension in the room. "Where'd you meet the kids?"

"Alice and Alex?" Akash didn't need to look around the man to know the twins hadn't stopped eavesdropping. They'd learnt the hard way to listen in on what people said about them. "They *are* family."

Before Hamish could respond, the twins burst into the kitchen. They threw their arms around Akash, crushing him in a hug between them. He turned his head to avoid a mouthful of hair.

They might put on a giddy and mischievous mask for the world, but Akash knew the twins struggled with not only their painful past, but being autistic as well. They trusted no one. He doubted anyone had ever treated them as a family should.

In the time Akash had known them, he and his family

had grown to care deeply for them. His mother often sent packages of treats, and the twins ate at his home frequently both in Cardiff and Fowey. Aside from a flat of his own, Alice and Alex had been the biggest change in his life since moving thus far, though he wondered if Hamish might change that.

Akash smiled apologetically at Hamish over the blond heads resting on his shoulders. "Grab a scone or two. I'll only be a moment."

Hamish nodded with a smile before stacking three of the freshly baked scones in his hands. "I'm good. Take your time."

With an arm around each sibling, Akash guided them out of the kitchen and awkwardly led them down the narrow hall into the office at the back of the building. Alice immediately took up her favourite spot on a worn leather chair in the corner. Alex sat on the edge of the desk, leaving Akash in the middle of the room; work meetings always wound up with them in the same positions.

Akash kept his eyes on the wall. Both of the twins were autistic. It affected them differently—but equally—and eye contact didn't come naturally to them. He suspected it was one of the reasons their parents had treated them so badly. Their earlier hug showed him how at ease they'd become with him. "Are you two doing all right? How about you take a break for a bit?"

Alice nodded. Alex shrugged. *So, yes.*

Akash moved over to his desk to turn on his Beatles playlist, which usually helped the two overwhelmed teens relax. "I'll manage the shop."

Leaving them to settle down, Akash returned to the kitchen

to find Hamish had already finished the three scones. The man smiled at him almost sheepishly, but casually grabbed a fourth from the nearby tray and started to nosh on it.

"Mind if we head out front? The twins are resting for a moment." Akash checked on the dough proving on the counter, glanced into the oven, and finally grabbed the remaining scones to take out to the displays. "Want another one?"

Hamish shook his head. "Think I've probably had enough. I have been tasked with bringing back half of the bakery. You're a sodding genius with spices. Best scone I've ever had, but don't tell my mum."

"Our secret."

For several minutes Hamish appeared content to watch him move around the shop, but eventually he broke the silence. "Would you be interested in going out with me for a meal? Maybe Friday or Saturday evening?"

Akash smiled brilliantly, but then his stomach dropped when he remembered his promise to his baby sister. *Damn.* "Funny you should ask."

Should I? Is it weird to invite him to a family meal? Shit. Is it? Okay. Stop blinking stupidly at him; he'll think you've sniffed too much saffron.

"Akash?"

A cheerful ding signalled a welcome interruption, and the arrival of customers. Akash wandered over, enjoying his temporary reprieve. It didn't last long.

Hamish had waited patiently until the customer exited the shop, only to prod Akash for an answer. "Well? Can I take you out?"

"Yeeeees—" Akash drew the word out.

"I sense a but."

Akash rubbed his hands on his apron when his palms suddenly dampened. *Spit it out.* "My little sister happens to be dating a friend of yours—Nye. She begged me to bring a date to our weekly family supper. How'd you feel about enjoying some authentic curry, invasive parental questions, and a trial by fire for our first date?"

"Sounds brilliant." Hamish's hand darted out, to snatch up a pasty this time. "I'll need my strength to be brave."

"Supper isn't until Friday. We have days to prepare." Akash couldn't help laughing at the idea of his diminutive mother terrifying the intense former Royal Marine.

Hamish eyed the various trays of baked goods in the store. "This will require careful planning, then."

Akash grabbed one of the nearby boxes and placed a selection of the pasties in it for the man. "You didn't ask about the twins?"

"We don't know each other well enough for me to pry." Hamish shrugged. "You're very kind to them—I was impressed. Not sure everyone would be so generous."

"You could see us through the open office door, couldn't you?" Akash sealed the box and handed it over to him while Hamish attempted to appear innocent. "They deserve better from the world. I help where I can."

It never feels like it's enough either.

CHAPTER SIX

AKASH

Freddie: Taine said to tell you Scottie might stop by this evening to ask you out.

   Akash: Why me?

   Freddie: Bad karma?

   Akash: Arse. How are you and the Tens machine doing? Done anything kinky lately?

   Freddie: Go dust the flour off your mobile.

   Akash: Use condoms.

   Freddie: Bite me.

   Akash: I'll leave that to Tens. Nighty night.

When Freddie didn't respond, Akash assumed his friend

had fainted from all the blood rushing to his head when he blushed. Taine would probably text him later to berate him for it. The man got rather tetchy when it came to his lover.

The warning about Scottie hadn't been completely necessary. Akash knew how to deal with bullies. His father had ensured all of his children were well versed in the art of self-defence; they'd all studied one form of martial arts or the other.

In fact, Akash had taken down larger idiots than Scottie in competition. *I've nothing to worry about.* Scottie might need to be concerned if he didn't get himself under control.

Alex and Alice made their escape early in the evening to work on their homework. Akash closed up the shop, prepped for the morning, and had just finished cleaning up when a hard knock rattled the rear door that connected the shop to the stairs leading up to his flat.

Broom in hand, Akash opened the door and found himself only mildly surprised to see Scottie standing with his arm still raised. They stared at each other in awkward silence. It had none of the ease Hamish brought with him.

Akash grew tired of the tense quiet. "Did you want something? Bakery closed an hour ago."

"Not here for fucking scones." Scottie appeared to be thrown by Akash's disinterested tone. "I'm taking you out to dinner."

"Was that a question?" Akash almost dropped the broom while staring at the overly confident man in front of him. "To quote my baby sister, 'um, like, no.'"

"Are you fucking turning me down? Me?" Scottie glanced

around as if expecting him to be talking about someone else. "Me? Are you fucking serious?"

Over the years, Akash's sisters had often complained about men refusing to gracefully accept rejection. He'd always wondered if they exaggerated. Scottie clearly proved their point.

The former rugby player practically frothed at the mouth over being turned down. His behaviour only made Akash more certain. He had zero interest in sharing even a coffee with the temperamental man.

"Are you fucking listening?" Scottie took a step toward him after having ranted for a good ten minutes. "Oi! Fucking—"

Akash brought the broom up quickly and used it to press Scottie back, cutting him off midsentence. "Not interested in whatever shite you're about to vomit on me. I find nothing attractive about you. *Nothing.* I'm not sodding interested."

Scottie couldn't seem to fully grasp what Akash said. "Are you fucking serious?"

Akash continued to use the broom to separate them. He had no idea what the volatile man might do, but had learned never to take chances. "Completely serious. Now get your *fucking* arse away from my door."

When Akash stepped back and turned to go inside, Scottie muttered a gay slur under his breath. The word hit like a ton of bricks. He started into the bakery only to stop and spin back around to face the man.

"One of these days, Scottie, you'll have to accept the fact that you're gay. I don't know what's caused this obvious self-hatred, but deal with it before you hurt someone." Akash slammed the door in Scottie's face. *I will not engage bullies and arseholes in conversation, particularly one who is obviously filled with self-loathing. It's pointless.* It had been one of the hardest lessons for him to learn. "Arse."

Setting the broom aside, Akash jogged up the stairs to his flat. He ran a bath while speedily scanning through his emails. A relaxing soak sounded like just the thing after his incredibly exhausting day.

Ganesh took up his usual post on the windowsill above the tub. The insane cat obsessively watched Akash whenever he bathed. He found it a tad disturbing; Shanti had only laughed off his concerns when he'd told her the first time it happened.

Arrogant assumptions aside, Akash struggled to process Scottie's complete lack of sensitivity. The man had insulted friends and strangers. He constantly picked fights, flinging slurs around like candy.

Resting his head against the edge of the tub, Akash tried to let the stress of the day to sink away. Hamish had been the bright spot, the only one. Ignoring troubles didn't come naturally to him; he preferred to face them head-on and immediately.

Akash had one major problem, aside from Scottie: the twins' stepfather. The man continued to harass the teens, albeit from a distance. They refused to talk to the police about it.

Contacting the police on their behalf wouldn't accomplish anything; the twins had reached adulthood. His hands were tied by their inaction. He'd already spoken to a friend of his who was a detective in London about it.

He mulled the problem over until the water turned tepid.

Ganesh had fallen sleep with his furry head dangling off the ledge. Akash's skin had turned clammy and wrinkly as the water cooled.

Time to get out.

With a towel wrapped around him, Akash wandered into the kitchen for some of the leftover pizza Alex and Alice had left in his fridge. He didn't have the energy to whip something up for himself. Cold pizza, a pint of whatever Jack had brought over last time they watched a rugby match together, and a few chapters in a novel while listening to the Beatles would be a brilliant way to end his evening.

One good thing to come out of day had been forgetting to stress over the family dinner. Akash did remember to text Shanti to tell her that Hamish had said yes and that she could repay the favour later. *Here's hoping this family dinner isn't a disaster.*

It wouldn't be.

His internal dramatics aside, Akash knew his parents to be loving and open-minded. When he wasn't panicking, logic told him that the chance of their being angry was slim to none. Fear still managed to creep into his heart.

His elder sister, Padma, on the other hand, might be a completely different story. She tended to take great pleasure in being as frustrating as she could to her younger siblings. Akash had mostly agreed to Shanti's plan in the hopes it would cut off any issues between the sisters.

Wishful thinking.

CHAPTER SEVEN

HAMISH

In the course of his military career, Hamish had, on occasion, walked into enemy fire to save one of the marines under his command. If that experience had been a ten on a scale of fear, heading into his office when everyone knew about his upcoming date shouldn't have even registered. Yet, here he stood, staring at the front door with a sense of foreboding.

Come on then, Hamish. Pull yourself up by your bootstraps, would you?

The morning would undoubtedly be chock-full of endless teasing. Hamish never played the field when it came to dating—unlike almost everyone in the office. None of them would miss an opportunity to harass a man they considered to be unflappable. Bracing himself, he opened the door and walked in.

Wyatt sat in his office, leaning back with the chair balanced on two legs and his feet propped against Hamish's desk. He had a report of some kind in one hand and a cup of coffee in the other. "I can hear you watching from the door, Hamster."

"Lying fuckwit." Hamish wondered if getting a smaller desk might stop everyone from putting their shoes on it. *Probably not.* "Any particular reason you're dirtying up my office?"

Wyatt waved the paper in his hand before throwing it on the desk and pulling out an American quarter. "Coin toss on who has to take this security job in South Sudan?"

"You're definitely a tosser." Hamish moved around the desk, snatching up the report and dropping into his seat with a groan. "Isn't it your team's turn to travel?"

"Technically."

He narrowed his eyes on the former Navy SEAL. "Why don't you just tell me why we're switching up the rotation instead of pulling out your trick coin?"

"Aled's mom is sick. He wants to travel to France to spend time with her and cook up some of his plant miracle shit. Voodoo's in New Orleans with his folks, Trace and Scorch want to climb some fucking mountain." Wyatt dropped his feet to the floor. "We'll take the next two—promise. My husband needs me, you know?"

In the seven years since they'd rescued the botanist on a boat in Anguilla, Hamish had enjoyed the pleasure of watching Wyatt and Aled fall head over heels in love with each other. No matter how strong the younger man might be, the Navy

SEAL could never quite seem to get beyond his need to be protective. Hamish didn't see a point in arguing about it.

I may as well save my breath and agree to it.

Hamish remembered when his own parents had died within months of each other—one from cancer and the other from a stroke. Wyatt and Aled had that sort of long-lasting relationship. "We'll manage. When are your lads back in the office? They'll have to cover some of the speaking engagements, since Lily and Vinnie will be coming with me."

"Not Nye?"

He shook his head before nodding toward the large calendar on the wall that everyone used to jot down their days off. "He blocked off the end of the month because he's testing out some new prosthetics for a robotics company."

"Oh?" Wyatt glanced up from where he'd been making notes on yet another report.

"Freddie put him in contact with this company. Nye's hoping to get even more use out of his arm in particular." Hamish hoped his friend would be able to recover better range and control. "Why don't we sort out the schedule this afternoon? Get everyone clear on who's doing what and going where, yeah?"

"Perfect." Wyatt bent forward with a calculating smile on his face. "Now, what's this I hear about you having a first date at a family dinner?"

Hamish turned his attention to the stack of files in front of him. "You can leave at any time."

"Chair's comfy."

He levelled a stony glare at the man; a warning Wyatt

completely ignored, of course. "I've no interest in adding fodder to the office gossip."

"You know we're only going to make shit up if you don't." Wyatt took a slow sip of his coffee. "Well?"

"Blackmail is illegal." Hamish sent a withering glare toward the man. "I'll give you one bit of information for every client email you handle."

"Fucking bastard."

"I am not. I've seen the photographs from my parents' wedding." Hamish dodged the file thrown at his head. "How about we both get to work?"

With much grumbling, Wyatt vacated the office. Hamish didn't believe for a moment the others wouldn't all find their way to his office to harass him. He opted for the cowardly way out by spending his day handling the long list of phone calls that had been put off for far too long.

By the end of the day, Hamish had accomplished more work than ever before, by simply trying to avoid being prodded for details. Wyatt still managed to smirk at him far too frequently. He planned to duck out of the office early for a much-needed drink at the nearest pub.

Maybe a pasty?

Too soon?

Akash does make genuinely good pies.

Oh, bloody hell, I've got it bad.

"Going to stop by after work?" Lily waltzed into his office with a mischievous grin on her face. She held out a fancily decorated tin. "Give him this."

"Why?"

"It's some sort of fancy tea. Traded for it with one of our contacts. It's expensive, and you can't buy it here." She shoved the box into his chest. "I badgered Freddie into finding out what Akash likes."

"Why?" Hamish asked for a second time.

"Will you trust me on this one? Please? He'll love the tea." Lily backed out of his office quickly. "Also, I'm leaving early."

Hamish snorted in amusement as she disappeared from view. "Of course."

Twisting the black and gold tin in his hand, Hamish inspected the intricate designs painted on it. He had a feeling it had cost her more than a favour. Lily had a tendency to bolt after any show of what might be emotion; something he usually avoided prying into.

Everyone deserves to have their secrets.

Canister of tea in hand, Hamish utilised all of his combat-honed skills to outmanoeuvre Wyatt and Nye to get to his vehicle. He hoped Akash wouldn't mind yet another impromptu visit. He didn't want to send the man running before they'd even managed a first date.

Let's hope the first isn't also the last.

In their type of work, Hamish often found himself gone for weeks or months at a time. He'd learnt the hard way to take advantage of the time available to him. Akash would hopefully be inclined to be patient with the occasional long-distance periods that a relationship with him would require.

As Hamish drove into one of the empty spots near the bakery, he almost immediately realised something had gone wrong. Hopping out of the vehicle and rushing up the pavement, he crunched over broken glass. Someone had shattered one of the large panes at the front of the shop.

"Hamish? That you?" Alex stood nearby, struggling to hold up a large piece of wood. "Can you give me a hand? We're trying to board up the window."

"What happened?" Hamish grabbed the thin wood and helped press it carefully against the remains of the window. "Someone take a brick to the window?"

"A cricket bat."

What?

"Did you say a cricket bat?" Hamish had to remind himself not to drop the wood while he blinked in surprise at the blond teenager. "Why? Do you know who did it? Is everyone all right?"

With quite a bit of stammering and fidgeting, Alex managed to explain how his and Alice's stepfather had decided to pay them all a visit. The man had taken the bat to one of the windows before Akash had managed to disarm him. Hamish was impressed. It appeared his baker had a few hidden talents, including a secret identity as a ninja, according to the teenager.

With a few gentle questions, Hamish learnt that Akash and Alice had gone to the police station to make their statements to detectives. As Alex hadn't seen it happen, he had stayed behind with a few university friends to clean up. Hamish opted to stay and give them a hand until his baker returned.

The baker.

The. Baker.

Not. Mine.

Not yet, anyway.

Bloody brain. Stop it.

After two hours of cleaning and fixing things, Hamish also gave a call to a mate of his who ran a glazing company. He promised to have someone out to repair the window first thing in the morning. It would be one less problem for Akash to stress over. Alex offered him a slightly watery smile by way of thanks.

"You know it's not your fault, right? All this shit." Hamish gestured toward the boarded-up window. "Your stepfather sounds like a real wanker. His actions aren't on your shoulders. He's a grown man who should know better."

"But…." Alex shrugged helplessly, clearly at a loss for words.

"Hamish has it right." Akash led Alice into the room with his arm around her shoulders. "Why don't you two head up to my flat to relax for a bit? I'm sure Ganesh could use the company—and you both look like you could do with a bit of peace and quiet. There's leftover takeaway in the fridge if you want it."

The twins trudged out of the room with their arms linked. Hamish stood awkwardly, a broom and dustpan still in his hands. He thought Akash might need a bit of quiet as well.

Hamish couldn't help watching Akash as he dealt with the twins. The baker seemed to have limitless patience with them. His eyes followed the man all around the bakery, slowly drifting down to focus on one particular part of his body.

He looks dead on his feet.

Right, do something useful then, aside from staring at how those jeans cling to his arse.

They look bloody amazing on him. Love to— Get your shit together, Hamish.

Deep breath.

You can't rip him out of his clothes. Not yet.

All of his deep breathing did nothing to assuage the way his cock hardened in his trousers. *Shit.* Hamish grasped desperately at the first non-sexual thought to cross his brain. It didn't work. He used his innate stubbornness to force his mind away from the delicious arse of the man in front of him.

"Oi. My eyes? Up here?" Akash snapped his fingers and snickered when Hamish jerked in surprise. "Thanks for staying with Alex."

Hamish waved off the thanks. He'd never even considered leaving the obviously uneasy teen alone. "How about we have a late supper together? If you let me borrow your kitchen, I could cook something up."

"You cook?"

"I'm no genius like you—but I can whip up something tasty." Hamish had taught himself how to cook after growing tired of takeaways. "I promise not to burn the place to the ground."

"Good. Not sure my insurance would cover it." Akash locked up the shop and gestured toward the door leading to the kitchen. "Go on then. Just don't give me food poisoning."

"Have a little faith."

CHAPTER EIGHT

AKASH

Drinking wine in his kitchen might not be a new thing, but having someone else cook for him certainly was. Akash took a sip of the sweet white wine and peered toward the pot on the hob. Hamish had handed him a tin of tea before turning his entire attention toward the meal.

Akash didn't mind the quiet. The afternoon had been far too chaotic for him. He hoped with the twins finally finding the courage to speak to the police that the dramatics with their stepfather would be over for good.

He'd keep his fingers crossed.

They'd scrounged around in the cupboards to find the ingredients for the dish Hamish wanted to make. It appeared they'd be having some sort of pasta. Akash happily allowed his stress to drift away in the warmth of his kitchen and the mellow wine.

Akash had discovered many years ago that he could learn a great deal from observing someone working with food. Hamish obviously enjoyed being organised and in control—if his concise *mise en place* meant anything at all. Military life had apparently left an impression on the man.

"You don't look even an eighth Italian." Akash had spent twenty minutes blatantly staring at the incredibly attractive man with his angular jaw covered in rough stubble, dark blue eyes almost hidden by his brow furrowed in concentration, and his greying blond hair. "Any reason you picked pasta?"

"A lazy lad's meal." Hamish grinned at him before reaching out to snag Akash's wine glass to steal a sip. "I did a tour overseas with a couple of Italians. They could make miracles happen with next to nothing for ingredients. I picked up a few tricks from them."

Akash narrowed his eyes on the man. "Ten quid says you googled a recipe on your mobile while I was in the loo."

Hamish took another drink before handing the glass back to him. "Found it online a couple of days ago."

"And you still remember it?"

"Eidetic memory." Hamish shrugged indifferently.

"Really?" Akash paused in pouring refills for both of them. "You've got a photographic memory?"

"Don't tell Wyatt. He's never figured out how I always fill out reports so quickly." Hamish's smile turned almost wolfish, and Akash felt weak in the knees—again. "Bit of a curse, at times."

"I'd give anything to never forget things. I've the worst memory in the world." Akash frequently left notes for himself and then lost them. "It'd be brilliant."

Hamish looked right through him, seeming miles away in thought. "No, you wouldn't want it. Never being able to forget an embarrassing moment? Or the worst time of your life?"

He paused to consider what it might be like to remember every single minute of each day. "*Shit.* I'd become a recluse."

"I've considered it."

Akash set the now full glass on the counter, just out of the way of the carefully arranged ingredients. "Why choose to join the military knowing you can never forget anything? I'd think you'd pick a safe career to avoid traumatising yourself."

Hamish tossed a few ingredients into the pan, stirring it before answering. "Family history."

"Your family served?"

"Not quite." Hamish made quick work of finishing up whatever the pasta was. "An uncle—my favourite one—died in a hijacking in the eighties. I watched on the telly while soldiers tried to rescue him. I decided I wanted to be one of them when I grew up."

"Most kids forget."

"I couldn't." Hamish tapped his nose with his finger. "How about you? Did you always want to make magic with dough?"

"Yes. No. Maybe?" Akash chugged down half his glass of wine. "It's a loaded question."

"Oh?" Hamish gestured to the simmering sauce. "I've got time."

"Family history." Akash tapped his fingers against the rim

of the glass for a few seconds. "Bakers run in the family. Not amongst the men, mind you. My father served in the military, as did his father and his grandfather. On my mother's side, they were all doctors or teachers going back generations."

"Not you?"

"Not me." Akash ran his fingers through his wavy black hair. "I had to be different."

"Nothing wrong with different." Hamish dipped a spoon into the sauce and held it out carefully toward him. "Want a taste?"

Akash bent forward to get a taste. He had to lick the sauce off his lips when it dripped from the spoon, smiling when Hamish immediately twisted away from him. *Like what you see, Mr. Marine?* "Not sure I believe you only found this recipe a few days ago."

It didn't take long for the rest of their supper to come together. Akash ran up two plates to the twins, only to find them asleep on his couch. He retreated quietly to the bakery's kitchen and found Hamish had already set up two chairs around one of the work tables.

They traded stories over their simple pasta dinner. Akash half expected the man to make a move—or to make one himself—but the evening had been too easy, too comfortable for it; they'd simply enjoyed the shared meal.

A sharp contrast to what Akash imagined a first date with Scottie might entail. The former rugby player had texted him four times since the night he'd stopped by uninvited, having stolen his number out of BC's phone. The persistence concerned him; he had no interest in having his life turned upside down by a stalker.

Making a mental note to apologise to his sisters for not taking their complaints about similar behaviour from other men more seriously, Akash had sent a text of his own earlier to Tens and Caddock. He knew them the best out of the rugby players involved with the Sin Bin. They'd sort out their mate, or he'd do it for them.

"Thanks for the tea." Akash gestured toward the tin sitting on the nearby shelf. "Do you know how bloody hard it is to get that particular type of tea? It's perfect for making biscuits."

"Right." Hamish was staring at him. He nodded absently, but didn't actually appear to have heard him.

"Something wrong?"

Standing abruptly, Hamish strode around the table to grab Akash by the shirt. He dragged him up out of his chair, causing him to stumble forward. Akash could only blink at the slightly taller man in confusion, until those wonderfully rough fingers dug into his hair and yanked him up into a kiss.

Akash surrendered to it briefly before bringing his arm up to separate their lips—and bodies—when Hamish's fingers drifted down the front of his shirt. "We're not doing this in my kitchen. Not yet. Well, not in the bakery kitchen, ever. Health inspectors would have a fit."

Hamish brushed his knuckles across the bulge in Akash's trousers. "Later, then?"

"Later when we're somewhere else and there aren't two nosy brats peeking through the door." Akash pointed toward the barely visible twins, who were once again eavesdropping on them. "Off with you both. I left you dinner on the table upstairs."

While the rest of the meal went well, the passionate moment had definitely passed them by. Hamish stayed for another hour, helping to wash up the dishes. They exchanged several heated kisses, until Akash had to quite literally shove the man out the door.

He sank back against the frame of the still open door to catch his breath after seeing Hamish off. "Well, bugger me."

"He fucking wants to."

Akash groaned when he spotted Scottie sitting on his motorcycle nearby. "What the bloody hell are you doing here?"

Scottie surged forward only to wind up on the ground, having stumbled over his bike. "Why the fuck won't you even give me a chance? Not asking for more than a date."

Akash couldn't help laughing at the idiot. "You're angry— all the time. You're a complete arsehole to everyone. Nothing about you says you're ready to date, let alone even contemplate a relationship."

"Fuck you."

Akash merely lifted his eyebrows at him. "No. Also, thank you for so eloquently proving my point. If you're so bloody tired of being alone, *Scott*, perhaps you might consider dealing with whatever has you so furious. You never know, it could help you keep some of your friendships before you lose them entirely."

"I—"

"I've dealt with enough angry arseholes for one day. Get yourself sorted or I'll report you." Akash stormed into his bakery and slammed the door behind him. "*Wanker.*"

CHAPTER NINE

HAMISH

How does one dress for a family dinner that is also a first date?

Well, the second, technically speaking. Dinner counts as a first date, right?

Hamish stood in front of his closet and stared at his clothing. He had all of it organised by use: work kit on the left, suits in the centre, casual to the right. A text from Nye cleared things right up for him: **Don't wear a tie or a jacket; you'll look like a right wanker.**

Helpful.

The encouraging texts continued to come in from all of

his friends. Hamish ended up turning off his mobile to ignore them. *Troublesome twats.* Revenge could come later; first, he had to decide what to wear that wouldn't make him "look like a right wanker."

Jeans and a button-up shirt it is.

Because of the distance between Cardiff and Fowey, where Akash's parents lived, they'd decided to meet for an early supper in Exeter. The city made a good halfway point for both groups. According to Nye, the three siblings usually travelled to their parents' homes once a month to stay for the entire weekend.

Tonight would be *special,* but hopefully not catastrophically awful.

Nye, Shanti, Akash, Alice, Alex, and Hamish would all be travelling together in his Mercedes GLS. It comfortably fit the entire group. He pulled onto the M5 and sent up a prayer for everything to go well.

The drive passed uneventfully for the first forty minutes. They had another hour or so to go, if traffic played nice. Hamish hoped to show up early to make a good impression on the Robinsons.

Hamish caught the sound of snickering from both twins behind him. He glanced over at Akash, who shrugged. "What's going on back there?"

"Oi. Stop snogging my sister." Akash had twisted around to see what had the twins laughing. He'd obviously spotted Nye and Shanti kissing in the back. "He's your employee—do something."

Hamish raised an eyebrow when the baker smacked him

on the arm. "She's your sister."

"The last time I told my baby sister what to do, she snuck dye into my shampoo bottle." Akash grinned ruefully at him. "Purple hair doesn't look brilliant on me."

Hamish shifted his hand over to rest on the man's knee. "Well, Nye's a slightly better shot than I am—even with half an arm missing. Also, he's as likely to listen to me as a brick wall."

"You've a better chance with the wall." Nye came up for air long enough to comment. "Don't be jealous that you're driving and can't engage in your own snogging."

The twins watched the banter between the four of them without comment. They appeared to find it all highly entertaining. Hamish let the conversation drop, though he kept his hand on Akash's knee.

"About my parents." Akash lowered his voice while the others continued nattering on in the back of the Mercedes. "They're lovely, you know, but still—parents."

Hamish gave the man's knee a squeeze. "Right. Not sure if you're trying to be encouraging or giving me a warning."

"Both?"

"Right."

Akash shook his head with an exasperated groan. "They want the best for their children in everything."

"And I'm not it?"

"A family dinner as a first date was a daft idea. What the bloody hell was I thinking?" Akash covered his face with his hands. "Bugger."

Hamish moved his hand from the baker's knee to rest

gently on his neck instead. He massaged the tight muscles while keeping his focus on the road ahead of them. "Dinner is only dinner with a few additions to the invitation list. Don't put so much stress on yourself, your parents, and whatever this is between us."

"Listen to him." Alex shoved his head between the driver and passenger seats. "It's just a bit of fun, right?"

"Right. I'm being irrationally dramatic." Akash murmured more to himself than the others, though Hamish heard him perfectly. "Irrational. They love me. Stop being idiotic."

The conversation drifted to lighter topics. Hamish allowed his stress about the meal to dissipate. He had some intense lust and definite interest in Akash invested into this connection thus far, but no deeper emotions.

If I repeat that to myself over and over, I won't feel as if my heart is in my throat and my stomach at the same time.

Dinner would be whatever it turned out to be. If it went badly, they could simply walk away with little more than mild disappointment. Hamish found himself hoping it went well.

Their drive out to Exeter progressed smoothly. The twins sunk into a whispered conversation together. Nye and Shanti continued their questionable activities in the back, right up to their pulling up in front of the restaurant.

Hamish got out of his vehicle, and walked around it until he could bang on the window next to Nye. He smirked when the couple jumped apart. "Time to meet the parents, lovebirds."

"Shouldn't you be more anxious?" Nye grumbled at him while the others slowly tumbled out of the Mercedes.

"I suddenly realised of the two of us, you've got more to

worry about than I do." Hamish locked the vehicle and turned toward the restaurant. "I mean, I'm not dating their youngest daughter. Not sure this distraction will work out quite like you hoped."

"Arsehole." Nye shoved him in the back with his prosthetic arm. "Is this your idea of being supportive?"

"Parent alert. Mummy, Papa, meet Nye." Shanti darted between them to grab her boyfriend by the hand and drag him over toward the older couple waiting nearby. Before either of her parents could respond, Shanti pointed them toward Akash. "He brought a date."

Hamish snorted in amusement at the blatant attempt at distraction. He couldn't deny it worked, since two matching intense glares switched over to him. He squared his shoulders instinctively at the scrutiny. "Mr and Mrs Robinson? It's a pleasure to finally meet you. I'm Major Hamish Ross."

"Major?" Akash's dad held his hand out, taking Hamish's in a hard, almost painful grasp. "Active duty?"

"Retired." Hamish met the man's grip with equal strength. "I understand you served as well."

"A lifetime ago, before this rabble ruled my life." Mr Robinson's entire face lit up when he looked at his children. "How long have you known my son?"

Hamish *almost* blanched at the question. "A few weeks."

"Ah." James Robinson shook his head with a laugh before releasing Hamish's hand. "Shanti enlisted you into her plan to distract us from the new man in her life."

Akash stepped up to intervene. "Papa—"

He waved off his son's attempt to distract him. "Your elder

sister couldn't help her interfering nature. She told us about Nye and Hamish two days ago."

From Akash's visible wince, Hamish got the idea his youngest sister wouldn't be pleased with their eldest sibling. As an only child, he'd never had to worry about someone ratting him out to his parents. He hoped the evening wouldn't devolve into arguing.

"You—come here." Akash's mother waved imperiously at Hamish to get his attention. She'd finished her interrogation of Nye, who had almost immediately disappeared into the restaurant with Shanti. "Well? Akash? Introduce us properly."

What's a sodding proper introduction?

Hamish found himself repeating his name and a slightly less intimidating handshake with the matriarch of the Robinson family. Her gaze pierced through his soul far more than her husband's had. He could readily understand why Nye had begged him to help mitigate his own first introduction.

"He'll do." She nodded once to her son before taking her husband's hand to walk up the path into the restaurant. "Akash, love, why do you let your sisters drag you into their messes? Really? Dinner with your parents doesn't make for a romantic first date. And how could you think we'd be bothered by your new man?"

Akash appeared lost for words for a moment before rushing over to wrap his arms around his mother, who whispered something to him that Hamish couldn't hear. "I love you."

"Such a silly boy. We've known since you were young." She patted his back while Akash's father stepped over to join the hug. "If we'd ever known it bothered you so, we would've broached the subject ourselves. We wanted to wait for you to get the courage to do it yourself."

"We'll be inside." Mr. Robinson squeezed his son's shoulder before leading his wife away.

"Don't be long and don't kiss on the pavement," she ordered sternly, though her eyes twinkled.

Hamish stared blankly at the couple disappearing into the restaurant. "Your mum could run the country."

"Too much paperwork. Mummy doesn't even like to write to-do lists." Akash smiled, his eyes a bit watery, before turning a glare toward a gleaming red Porsche that had pulled up. Hamish could see that underneath everything else, his date was relieved at how his parents had accepted him. "Well, prepare yourself for fireworks. I'd wager Shanti's going to have words with Padma before the pudding."

"You going to be okay?"

"Definitely." Akash rubbed his eyes roughly with his shirtsleeve. "I should've talked to them about this in private ages ago and not by bringing a date to dinner. I was afraid, and now it's over, I'm not even sure why I was so terrified. I should've told them, though. There never seemed to be a perfect time."

Hamish wrapped an arm around Akash's shoulders and gave a comforting squeeze. "Life is never perfect."

All of his assumptions regarding Akash's parents proved to be entirely false. Hamish found the entire family to be rather lively. His mum and dad had been far more reserved.

Indira and James Robinson wore their hearts on their sleeves, and they'd apparently passed down this trait to their two youngest children. Padma, the eldest, appeared to be the most serious of the family. Hamish got the feeling she had a slight chip on her shoulder as a result.

The fireworks between the sisters waited until their entrees had been served. Shanti carefully set her knife and fork to the side. She glared across the table at her sister, while Akash cautiously reached out to pick up his glass of wine and leant away from the table with it in hand.

"Bombs away?" Hamish whispered to the man, who nodded with a wry smile. "Should I have worn Kevlar?"

Padma glanced absently down at her nails as if she didn't care about what her sister was saying. "Just because you can't be bothered to talk about anything important with our parents, doesn't mean I don't. They deserved to know about this man you're trying to saddle yourself with."

"You had *no* right." Shanti practically vibrated with anger in her chair. "You're always shoving your nose in my business. You've never met Nye. What gave you the right to tell anyone about him? He's my boyfriend. You *always* do this."

"Always? Hardly." Padma scoffed at her younger sister. "What about you? Throwing a tantrum because I'm honest with our parents?"

"Honest? Honest. You're joking, right? You're not being *honest* with Mummy and Papa. You're using a little bit of knowledge to needle me in front of them." Shanti shot to her feet, and only a quick movement from Nye kept her chair from falling over. "It's what you always do. You pick at Aki and me whenever you get it into your mind that we might have something you don't. Jealous cow."

Mrs Robinson rapped her knuckles on the table. "No name calling, Shanti. You can use your words without resorting to childish insults."

"Yes, Mummy." Shanti turned her head to the side to stick her tongue out at her sister. "It's still true. She's just jealous."

Hamish tuned out the argument briefly to watch the reaction of the elder Robinsons. The parents appeared content to allow their children to settle the fight amongst themselves. He'd thought they would've intervened by now, if only because of the relative strangers present.

Padma's voice rose with each word. "Jealous? Of what? You're banking on your looks and a passing knowledge of design to—"

"Padma." Akash spoke softly, but his voice held an impressive amount of weight. "Is now the time?"

"And you—" She quickly turned her ire toward him.

Akash folded his arms across his chest and relaxed into the chair. His manner surprised Hamish. "Yes? Share your vaunted wisdom about how my life could be going so much better. Never mind my successful bakery; never mind the attractive man sitting beside me. What am I doing wrong this week? Why can you never be proud of your own accomplishments without also deriding mine and Shanti's at the same time?"

His son stepping into the arena apparently signalled to James Robinson that the time had come to an end the argument. Akash's father smoothly interrupted his children by lifting his glass to offer a toast to the newcomers at the table. Hamish and Nye exchanged wry smiles before graciously acknowledging the kind gesture.

"Are your parents always so keen to allow their children to battle it out?" Hamish waited until the rest of the table had moved on to turn to his date. "Mine would likely have squashed it immediately."

"They enjoy a healthy debate." Akash sipped his own drink, and glanced apologetically over at Hamish. "Not a boring first date, is it?"

Hamish chuckled at the sheepish-sounding man who'd so confidently berated his sister moments earlier. "Most interesting one I've ever had."

"Well, that's something."

CHAPTER TEN

AKASH

Dinner ended relatively well. Between his sisters sniping at each other and a slightly raucous drive back to Cardiff, Akash failed to get more than a moment alone with Hamish. He found himself alone in his apartment with Ganesh, and collapsed on the sofa, barely remembering to kick off his shoes, allowing the exhaustion of the night to overtake him.

As the twins had promised to arrive early on Saturday, Akash dozed through the first three warnings from his phone alarm. He eventually stumbled into the bathroom with his eyes closed, and promptly tripped over Ganesh. The cat yowled indignantly at him and darted across his bare feet.

Ganesh scratched his leg on the way out, causing Akash to skid on the carpet. He caught his foot on the edge of the cabinet and pitched head first into the tub. His head hit the tap while the rest of his body bounced against the unforgiving edges of the porcelain.

"Bugger." Akash lay on his back in the tub with a bruised arm, side, and arse, along with a gash across his forehead. "Bloody sodding cat. Trying to kill me before I've had coffee."

Stretching his arm out, Akash managed to snag the edge of the nearby towel to drag it off the rod, and pressed it to his forehead. *Death by cat. How humiliating.* His mobile went off, but he ignored it. Not five minutes later, his door buzzer sounded. He dragged himself up out of the tub, and made his way down to the main door that led up to his apartment over the bakery. He still wore the clothing from the previous night, along with the towel still pressed to his head. Hamish stood outside waiting for him with two cups and a paper bag in his hands. "Morning."

Hamish's eyes widened when he spotted the towel in Akash's hand. "Are you all right? What the hell happened?"

Before Akash could actually respond, Hamish caught him by the arm to guide him up the stairs into his flat. He set the cups and bag on the table by the door before dragging Akash further inside by the wrist until they reached the bathroom. He had no choice but to allow the former Royal Marine to tend to his wound.

Pushy bastard.

"How on earth did you manage this?" Hamish firmly pressed the towel to the cut. "Do you have a first aid kit anywhere? Nothing bleeds like a head wound."

"My first aid kit is in the bottom of the cabinet. As for how it happened, I tripped over Ganesh." Akash couldn't help the slight flush on his cheeks when Hamish chuckled. "Don't be an arse. I'm all banged up from tumbling into the tub."

"You tripped over a god? In your bathroom?" Hamish caught him by the chin and tilted his head slightly while holding up two fingers. "How's your vision? Seeing any spots?"

Akash knocked the hand out of his face. "My cat, you twit. My sister named him Ganesh."

"Oh."

Akash nodded to the cat sauntering into the room to rub against Hamish's legs. "What are you up to?"

"Me? Or the cat?" He gently moved Ganesh out of his way and bent down to retrieve the first aid kit. "I'll assume you're talking to your feline friend."

Neither cat nor man appeared moved by Akash's glare. He deeply regretted not waking up when his first alarm had gone off. It might've prevented this mildly humiliating experience, though he didn't necessarily mind having Hamish's hands on his body.

Even if he's sopping up blood and patching up my wound. Sodding cat.

Why is he here anyway?

"Do you make a habit of randomly showing up without an invitation? I'm starting to wonder, as it's the third time. What're you doing here?" Akash led Hamish into the living room, where he retrieved the cups and bag left on the table. "Actually, more importantly, what've you brought me?"

"Some kind of weird tea blend that the bloke at Waterloo

Tea swore by—and a Welsh rarebit croissant." Hamish plucked one of the pastries out of the bag before casually tossing it to Akash. "I meant to chat with you last night about something, but the evening got away from us."

"Supper went better than I thought, aside from the brief sisterly fireworks." Akash took a tentative sip of the tea, only to be pleasantly surprised by the delicious taste. "You sure you can't remember the name of this? It's brilliant. I bet I could make the best biscuits out of it."

"Not a clue." He dug around in his pockets and finally found a carefully folded piece of paper. "Hibiscus Berry."

They finished their breakfast in relative silence, Hamish appearing to be struggling to find the right words. Akash gave him all the time he needed. He focused instead on what type of biscuit might go best with the fragrantly floral tea as its base.

Always testing the boundaries with his baking, Akash prided himself on bringing new and fresh ideas into the bakery. He'd built a reputation on it. They might have to do an entire series of tea-inspired treats.

Akash drained the last of his drink, and decided he'd been patient enough with waiting for the conversation to start. "Are you here for a particular reason? Aside from patching me up from my morning stupidity?"

Hamish tapped his fingers against the edge of his cup. "I mentioned how we travel with charities to provide logistical support and security."

"Right." Akash ran his fingers through his hair before folding his arms lightly across his chest. He couldn't figure out where the former marine might be going with the conversation; a baker wouldn't offer much assistance with either logistics or security. "Sorry. Why?"

"I'd wanted to ask you out again, only I'll be leaving next week." Hamish focused tired blue eyes on Akash. "Can I email you?"

"Pardon? Can you email me?" He blinked a few times to process the question. "Are you asking if you're capable, or if I want to hear from you while you're sun tanning in some desert somewhere? Not sure I can help you with IT support."

"The latter." Hamish gave the deep sigh of someone used to being teased. "Want to be my pen pal?"

"You're an idiot." Akash didn't even bother to hide his laughter. "Aren't we too old to play pen pals?"

"Sexting?"

Akash choked on his own saliva at the deadpan way Hamish made the suggestion. He coughed to clear his throat. "Why don't we start with regular messages and see where it goes, yeah?"

"Have any plans for today?" Hamish swirled his tea around before taking another sip from the cup. "Want to go for a walk in one of the nearby parks with me?"

Akash opened his mouth to say no—he did have work to do—but found himself agreeing instead. "Just let me get changed and talk to the twins. They can handle the shop for a few hours without me."

Making his way toward the bedroom, Akash found himself caught and dragged toward Hamish, who sat on the arm of the couch with his legs spread to allow Akash to stand between them. Inner thighs pressed tightly against outer ones while they stared at each other.

"Bit hard to get changed out here." Akash struggled to keep his voice steady.

"Shall I help? Marines are dedicated to assisting their fellow man." Hamish smirked at him before reaching out to start unbuttoning the shirt Akash had worn the previous night. His fingers strayed along the swaths of bare chest revealed. "Perhaps you'd be kind enough to send me away with a few memories to keep me warm at night."

The shirt fell easily off his shoulders. Akash hissed when Hamish ran his fingers lightly over the bruised skin from his earlier fall. He glared at the grin from the man who'd moved on to slowly undoing his belt.

Bloody hell.

This is slow torture.

And a bit much when we've barely gotten to what could loosely be considered one date.

"A bit soon, isn't it?" Akash dropped a hand down to cover the fingers toying with the button on his trousers. "We've yet to manage an actual first date with just the two of us."

"I brought tea—twice." Hamish didn't attempt to free his hands, though he bent forward to press his lips against one of the bruises on Akash's side. "How about I take you out for our first 'just us' date?"

Akash gazed down at the blond who couldn't seem to resist laying a path of kisses along his abdomen. *Bloody hell. He's got my knees going weak.* "Let me hop in the shower and get washed up."

"Want a hand?" Hamish moved his hands up to splay them against Akash's sides. "I'm rather skilled at jobs that require thorough and careful handling."

"I'm sure you are." Akash drew on his many years of martial arts to force himself to take a step back from the intoxicating man. "I've already fallen in the tub once today. Not sure I could handle a second tumble."

"You could always think of it as a descent controlled by an expert." Akash couldn't help licking his lips, and Hamish's blue eyes visibly darkened. "If you're sure?"

"I'm sure."

I'm not.

"Believe the bath is over there." Hamish pointed toward it when Akash failed to move. "You don't seem sure."

Move your damned feet, Akash.

CHAPTER ELEVEN

HAMISH

Hamish never slept in beyond nine in the morning. *Ever.* Even as a child, he tended to rise earlier than his parents most days. He'd woken early, as always, and the temptation to visit Akash had been impossible to resist.

He'd dithered around his flat for almost two hours before finally caving to the desire. Akash wouldn't mind another surprise visit. *I hope.* The baker hadn't seem bothered by his previous ones.

Why does he bring this out in me?

Along with patience, life in the Royal Marines had taught him to approach things methodically. Rash decisions didn't come naturally to him, and stopping for tea and croissants had definitely been a last-minute decision. He hoped his idea to walk in the park before stopping for lunch would be as well received.

Apparently a good one.

All of his attention was currently focused on a single, dull rectangle. Hamish stared at the closed bathroom door for almost twenty minutes. His mind created vivid images of the man on the other side of it.

Hamish finally gave in to the need to squeeze his already hard cock through his jeans. "This is *not* conducive to a hike in the park."

Unless the walk becomes a euphemism for something more fun and more naked.

Definitely naked.

Over the years, Hamish had dated a variety of men from different walks of life and ethnicities. He tended to go for confident and stoic types. Most of his relationships lasted for years, as opposed to weeks or months, unlike Wyatt, who had suffered from relationship ADD before meeting Aled.

When Hamish had been introduced to Akash the first time, he'd immediately found him attractive. *Lust before anything else as always, but I've always held out for something deeper.* The more they chatted with each other, the stronger his fascination grew. He only hoped his trips overseas didn't turn the man off.

It might actually end up being a blessing in disguise. The two would hopefully continue to develop a close relationship via text. He'd always found the journey from friendship to lover to be a satisfying one.

Not having to deal with interference from friends and

family also appealed to him. He wouldn't have to hear the constant nattering from Wyatt and the others—although it wouldn't save Akash from teasing.

Ah, well.

Wonder if he needs help drying off?

Resisting the urge to snoop around the small flat, Hamish made himself comfortable on the sofa. He stretched his long legs out, only to laugh when the long-haired tabby cat hopped up onto his lap. The creature purred up a storm while Hamish threaded his fingers through the soft fur.

"Ganesh will cover you in long strands of cat fur," Akash warned. He sauntered by in nothing but a towel on his way to what must've been his bedroom. "I'll only be a moment."

"Drop the towel, and you can take all the time in the world." Hamish inhaled sharply when Akash turned the teasing back on him by releasing the covering as he walked out of the room. It gave him a flash of delectable, bronzed arse. "You're a rude lad."

"Says the man still staring at my arse." Akash grinned over his shoulder and continued into his room. "No wanking on my couch."

Hamish had never imagined the quiet and calm demeanour of the baker hid such a teasing minx. He willed his hard-on away by reciting the times table. It usually worked like a charm.

Not today.

Shit.

The opportunistic Ganesh chose that moment to jump out of his lap. Hamish launched himself off the sofa with a shout when the cat's claws dug into his tender bits. He glared at the menace, who merely hissed angrily at him.

Rubbing his suddenly sore and shrunken cock gently, Hamish cursed under his breath. *This doesn't look odd at all.* It hurt almost as badly as the time he'd taken a rifle to the groin on a mission overseas. The cat merely spun around and traipsed out of the room, flicking his tail.

"What the sodding hell is going on out here?" Akash rushed out clad in boxers and a T-shirt, only to skid to a halt. His eyebrows rose practically to his hairline when he noticed Hamish still rubbing himself. "Not sure I even want to know."

"Your cat has claws," Hamish muttered petulantly. He couldn't recall being this close to blushing in his life. "Painful. Claws. Very. Painful."

"Yes, he does. I'm guessing the claws found their mark." Akash had his lips pressed tightly together as if trying to suppress a laugh. "Is the massage helping?"

Hamish closed his eyes and heaved a heavy sigh. "Just… get dressed. Please?"

"Want ointment?" Akash seemed quite content to stay to watch. "You might have to drop your trousers for that to work better."

"Perhaps." He sent a withering glare at Akash, who chuckled before returning to finish dressing. Hamish couldn't help offering a final retort. "You could always kiss it better for me."

Three days.

Three dates.

Three long goodbyes with addictive kisses and seductive touches.

Their walk along part of the River Taff rolled into a late lunch. Hamish spent the rest of the afternoon hanging out at the bakery. He enjoyed relaxing in the warmth of the shop and watching Akash in his element.

The baker worked like a master magician with flavours and spices. Hamish could throw a simple meal together. He'd never watched someone so skilled; the passion reminded him of his own drive when it came to weapons, risk assessment, and combat expertise.

Wyatt came by in the afternoon to drag him away. They had meetings to prepare for the upcoming trip. Hamish spent most of the time thinking about spending Sunday with Akash.

And I've lost what's left of my mind.

He did end up spending most of Sunday with Akash. It played out almost identically to Saturday, only without the unwelcome interruption of his friends. The evening ended with a curry and *The Great British Bake Off*, a show his baker insisted was the best thing on telly.

They'd said their goodbyes over lingering kisses. Akash hadn't been ready to move into the bedroom, and Hamish respected his wishes. He'd never been one to push a relationship faster than it needed to go.

Resigning himself to not seeing the man for months, Hamish spent his Monday wrapping up all the last-minute details. Their contract with the non-profit organisation for this trip was thankfully one of the shorter ones—only two months, with potential to extend for an additional one. He was pleasantly surprised when Akash showed up with a packed lunch.

Former military operatives whispering and giggling made Akash laugh, and Hamish pinched the bridge of his nose in frustration. He had no doubts he'd end up under massive scrutiny once the baker swanned off. The only downside to the large glass walls that blocked off their individual offices was they couldn't do anything more than chat.

"So—email me, yeah?" Akash stood hesitantly in the alley leading to the parking garage. "Text me? Something?"

Hamish caught him by the waist and walked him backwards until Akash bumped against the wall. He slid his hands up along his sides before resting one on the slightly shorter man's shoulders and gripping him firmly by the neck with the other. "Will you miss me?"

Deciding not to give Akash time to respond, Hamish lowered his head until their lips met. He immediately darted his tongue out for a taste. *God, how am I going to go months without this?* They kissed until Wyatt wandered past and wolf-whistled.

Tuesday came far too quickly. After much debate amongst the others, Hamish ended up flying out with Lily and Vinnie. They'd hit the tarmac at Heathrow before sunrise. He prepared himself for several long weeks of unsatisfying emails.

How long would several months really be? Hamish hadn't minded waiting—not entirely. He'd always believed intimacy to be a healthy part of a relationship, but not immediately hopping into bed wouldn't kill him.

There's always email.

And wanking.

So much wanking. Should've brought lotion.

CHAPTER TWELVE

AKASH

Hamish: Hello.

Akash: Hello.

Five minutes seems a long break for a text message. Maybe he's busy?

Hello. Hello? That's the best I could do for a greeting. I'm hopeless and doomed to loneliness and misery.

Hamish: Bit awkward, isn't it?

Akash: A bit.

Akash: All right, it's more than a little awkward.

Hamish: Could be worse. We could be shit conversationalists with an audience of friends to laugh at us.

Akash: Fair point. How's Sudan?

Hamish: Quiet at the moment. Started your day yet?

Akash: You caught me as I was about to step into the shower.

What the hell do the dots mean? What's he thinking? It's been two minutes. Say something.

Hamish: Sorry. I'm visualising you without your clothes on, and it's a breathtaking image.

Akash: You've a rather vivid imagination.

Hamish: You could always take a photo to allow me to decide for myself.

Hamish: Damn. Have to cut this short. Docs are ready to head out. Think about me while you're in the shower.

I am a sodding moronic twit.

I could've slept with a man built like a Roman warrior, with the chiselled jaw, abs, and everything else.

Did I?

No.

Sodding. Moronic. Idiot.

The emails started off more innocently than their text messages. They played journalist and interviewed each other. Hamish sounded a bit too comfortable in the role of interrogator; not surprising given the nature of his training and work.

They flirted.

Constantly.

A month into Hamish being gone, their exchanges took a different tone. Flirtation moved from subtle to blatant. Akash spent an uncomfortably embarrassing amount of time with his laptop and a hand down his pants.

Hamish: You up?

Akash: You're only two hours ahead of me—of course I'm up, it's six in the sodding morning. Shouldn't you be working?

Hamish: Late morning for the doctors so I'm resting while I can.

Akash: Find any spiders in your bunk?

Hamish: Tell Wyatt that he's a dead man when I see him again.

Akash: Speaking of your American, I've seen either him or one of his buddies at least every other day since you left. Something you want to tell me?

Hamish: Your pastries are incredibly addictive.

Akash: Right.

Hamish: Your kisses are fairly addictive, as well. They've been on my mind constantly.

Akash: Don't they teach you marines better methods of diversion?

Hamish: If I were there, you wouldn't be able to think of anything other than my lips on your skin.

Akash: Mildly better attempt.

Hamish: Would it be better if I explained in explicit detail what I plan to taste?

Akash: Definitely.

Akash: As I'm already late, it'll have to wait until later.

Hamish: You tease. I'll be sure to email you later.

Akash: Be safe, yeah?

Hamish: Always.

Every morning for the last two weeks had begun in the

same manner, with a playful text conversation. Akash found himself slowly building a new routine around the moments he chatted with Hamish. He thanked any gods who cared to listen for the fact South Sudan happened to be only a few hours ahead, and not in some random time zone requiring him to be awake at odd hours of the day.

Dragging himself off the couch, Akash set his empty mug from breakfast in the sink, and headed into the shower. He opted for a cold one to hopefully wake himself up. The twins wouldn't be in until later so he had a long morning ahead of him; he really had to hire another assistant.

I'll give the catering department at Cardiff and Vale College a call. They might have a few students who can work as an assistant. They can always fit in around the twins and save me from exhausting myself and maybe one'll be able to manage the shop on their own to give me more time off to live.

After getting his second batch of baked goods in the oven, Akash opened up the bakery. Not five minutes later, Trace strolled into the shop. *Oh, honestly.* What did they think would happen in Hamish's absence?

"Did you draw the short straw today?" Akash watched in amusement while the American perused all the baked goods. "Allow me to help things along. I've not gone anywhere, and you'll want to order, and I quote 'the pasty pastry things without the weird meat.' And for the record, lamb and goat aren't weird meats to a vast majority of the world."

"Goat's weird." Trace made a show of glancing at anything *but* what they usually ordered. "Might want something different."

"Do you?" Akash challenged teasingly.

"No." Trace grinned unapologetically. "Have you heard from Captain Britain?"

"Who?"

"The Hamster."

"Ahh, Hamish." Akash levelled a glare at the muscled former SEAL, who continued to grin innocently at him. "I've no doubt that he's contacted you several times."

"Probably." Trace shrugged. "What about you?"

Akash finished packaging up the baked goods for the man. He threw in a few extras for the others in the office. "Fifteen quid."

Trace appeared to find his reticence to gossip about Hamish admirable, and fished out the money quickly. "Don't worry too much about the Hamster. He knows how to keep himself alive."

Akash almost dropped the box of pastries in his hand. "Is this your way of comforting me?"

"Nah. Comfort isn't really my thing." Trace offered him a teasing salute, and sauntered toward the door of the bakery with a parting shot. "We're sending a package off to them. Want to add something? Lotion? Naked photos?"

"Go away now." Akash refused to dignify the nonsense with a response. "Idiot."

His day went by as it always did, with a revolving carousel of flour, spices, customers, clean up, and more baking. The monotony of his routine usually appealed to Akash. His mind often created the most unusual flavour combinations when distracted by the mundane.

Not today, it seems.

He didn't enjoy any of it, not even a little. Questions rolled around in his mind, distracting him completely. He'd overproved a batch of rough puff pastry, and burned an entire tray of curried raisin scones until they closely resembled hardened lumps of coal; they'd almost caught fire.

Well, bugger.

What's wrong with me?

The twins kept sending confused glances his direction. Akash finally decided to close the bakery an hour early and sent them home to study. He finished up leftovers from the meal his auntie Jenny had brought with her when she and his uncle came to visit earlier in the week.

He fell asleep on his couch for the thousandth time with Ganesh purring on his chest. Like every night of the past few weeks, he tossed and turned endlessly, unable to rest. He woke up at two to drink his way through a bottle of wine and try to avoid messaging Hamish.

He failed.

From: akash@robinsonbakery.co.uk

Date: Wednesday, 06 September, 2017 at 03:14:31 +0100

To: HamishRoss@HRSP.co.uk

Subject: Three in the sodding morning.

And I'm up, half-hard, thinking about you.

I might've had some of the wine left over from Jack and Graham's visit. Think you'll be home by November? My auntie Jenny and uncle Matt always throw this family meal to celebrate my parents' anniversary. Every sodding year they ask if I'm seeing anyone.

We're seeing each other.

Right?

Yes.

So, I'm up at whatever it is in the morning, cock out, worrying that you might not like me.

It's pathetic.

I'm not sending this.

On second thought, I am sending it because you're in South Sudan and can probably use a laugh.

Akash

From: HamishRoss@HRSP.co.uk
Date: Wednesday, 06 September, 2017 at 06:14:31 +0300
To: akash@robinsonbakery.co.uk
Subject: Morning Sunshine.

Heading out in five, so I've only a minute for a few important details that you should definitely keep in mind.

- I do like you.
- You're not pathetic.
- Get some rest. No burning your bakery down from lack of sleep.
- Hands off your cock. I'll reward you later if you manage to restrain yourself.

Hamish

CHAPTER THIRTEEN

HAMISH

October dawned in Juba bright and early. As jobs went, this had gone relatively smoothly thus far. None of the local troublemakers had made an attempt to interfere with the doctors, which made his job a breeze.

As the man in charge of the security unit, Hamish never truly relaxed—too much rested on his shoulders. His mind still found too much time to think about things *not* related to safety. His thoughts always drifted to Akash like a compass needle sought truth north; no amount of shaking dislodged it for more than a second or two.

Long-distance relationships in his line of work generally turned out to be terrible ideas. Hamish had initially thought his flirtation with Akash might fail before it had a chance to flourish, but that hadn't been the case. Each email, text, or Skype conversation with the man made him hungrier for the next.

Over their many weeks of constant text conversation, they'd delved deeper into each other's souls than if they'd been dating in person. Some secrets still had to be shared. Hamish hoped Akash felt as drawn into the hope of a relationship as he did.

The doctors wanted to be home before Christmas. Hamish had no complaints. The sooner they returned to England, the quicker he could get his hands—and mouth—on Akash.

One quick text can't hurt before I check in with Isaac.

Hamish: Morning, sunshine.

Hamish: Might be home by December, if the docs don't try extending their visas. They said they won't.

Akash: Excellent. I have plans.

Hamish: Plans? What plans?

Akash: You'll have to wait and see.

Hamish: Patience is my middle name.

Akash: Bit odd.

The teasing conversation continued until Lily stuck her head in to tell him to get moving. Hamish ignored her pointed look. Things were going too brilliantly to be ruined by a bit of teasing.

Maybe too brilliantly.

As a lad, Hamish's dad always cautioned him on complacency. *Life always surprises you, lad. When you're all comfy and happy, it's got a way of reminding you to never take anything for granted.* He tried to live with those words as his guide.

Stepping out into the bright sunlight, Hamish heard a high-pitched squeak. He tried to dodge the scurrying creature that his boot had almost crushed. It went left while he wavered toward the right.

"Oh, shit." Hamish pitched forward when his ankle turned, and tumbled shoulder first into the hard-packed soil. He twisted around carefully onto his back while breathing deeply through the sudden and intense pain. "Bloody mouse."

"What the hell did you do to yourself?" Vinnie squatted by his head. "You all right?"

"Been better."

One dislocated shoulder later, the doctors forced Hamish to make the decision to head home far earlier than intended. They'd managed to put the bone back into the socket, and he likely wouldn't need surgery, but he'd be in a sling for at least a week—and unable to return to full capacity for a month or so.

During his military service, Hamish had dislocated his shoulder twice. He knew how to care for it. His body tended to take six to seven weeks to heal; he had no reason to think this would be any different.

Lily and Vinnie took immense joy in teasing him over being felled by a humble dormouse. Hamish ignored it, along with their comments on the orders for no strenuous activity until his doctor in Cardiff x-rayed the injury. *Why do I put up with their nonsense?*

Hamish: I've good news and bad news.

Akash: Oh?

Hamish: Good news: I'll be in Cardiff by tomorrow evening.

Akash: Well, that's a surprise. What's the bad news?

Hamish: I'v*e managed to dislocate* my shoulder.

Akash: Poor lad. How'd you do it?

Hamish: Tripped over a dormouse.

Akash: Pardon me while I die of laughter.

Hamish: **Your lack of sympathy has been noted, particularly since you tripped over your cat.**

Akash: Sorry. Can't type. Laughing myself silly.

Hamish: Eve ryone's got jokes for me.

By the time Hamish touched British soil, almost every single friend had reached out to him. He scrolled through all of the messages while the plane taxied toward the gate. Arses. Who needs them. Lily and Vinnie had obviously been busy telling everyone how he'd managed to injure himself. He sent one group text in response.

Hamish: Thanks for all the kind encouragement.

Hamish: Wankers. Also, Earp, talk to Lils and Vinnie to see if they can handle the last little bit in Sudan without backup.

Going to his flat alone and sore didn't appeal to him, but what other option did he have? Hamish forced himself to make the journey. The idea of a solitary evening caused his mood to plummet even further. He regretted not listening to the doctor in Juba about the level of pain from the injury; his general disdain for strong pain medication had backfired on him.

I hurt.

I'm hungry.

I can't lift more than a piece of paper, let alone fix myself a decent meal.

The cab driver had been kind enough to run into the shop to pick up a few things for him. The man had taken one look at Hamish and generously offered to lug his bags up for him as well. He tripled the fare by way of thanks.

Cooking one-handed turned out to be harder than it sounded. Hamish grimaced at his attempt at comfort food; a fry-up had been a brilliant plan until it congealed into a mess in the pan. The shrill ring of his doorbell drew his attention from the culinary nightmare.

"Good evening." Akash smiled cheekily at him when he opened the door. "One of your mates mentioned you'd be home alone, all starved and morose. I brought food. We can't have a national hero suffering in silence."

Hamish decided not to pay any attention at all to the sudden flash of warmth in his body. He also ignored the teasing prod at his mood. "Hello, then."

"Going to invite me inside?" Akash lifted the lid on the container in his hand, offering Hamish a whiff of delicious spices. "My mum swears this makes everything better—not quite sure it works on dislocated shoulders. I imagine it's loads better than whatever you've managed to throw together."

"Dodgy eggs." Hamish shrugged and immediately regretted the move. "*Bugger.*"

"Maybe avoid hurting yourself further?" Akash followed him into the flat and went straight into the kitchen to make himself at home. He plated up what looked like shepherd's pie but smelled like a curry. "How starved are you?"

"Ravenous."

Akash glanced over his shoulder at him. "Keep it in your trousers. I'm certain the doctor didn't approve you for anything other than rest."

"Spoilsport."

"Eat your supper." Akash carried the plates over to the table and set them down. "Or shall I spoon-feed you?"

"I'll feed you something." Hamish glared at him, only to be smacked in the face with a pea. "I'm ill-equipped for war at the moment."

"You'll have to return the favour later." Akash winked at him before returning to his own meal. "Eat."

"Yes, sir."

CHAPTER FOURTEEN

AKASH

While the concept of playing nursemaid to a Royal Marine brought all sorts of erotic thoughts to his mind, Akash found the actuality of it to be far less smutty. They sat on the sofa and watched nonsense on the telly. Their supper warmed their bellies and left them in a dozy state.

He briefly considered taking Jack's advice to go a more direct route. All the time apart had only solidified his growing desperation to discover what might come after the heated kisses they'd exchanged. Hamish's injury would limit them to little more than kisses until he could move without wincing.

Stubborn arse who refuses to take anything to feel better. Honestly.

"If you're going to curse my stupidity, do it out loud."

Hamish turned knowing eyes toward him. He stretched his legs out to rest on the sofa. "I'm impressed you've managed not to take the mickey over my tripping over a mouse."

"Thought you might feel bad enough as it was." Akash couldn't keep his lips from turning up into a broad grin. "Honestly though, a mouse? How the hell did you manage to trip over a little creature in South Sudan? I mean, of all the scary things I imagined happening to you, none of it included you falling over your own feet."

Hamish grunted in pain when he attempted to twist around in an obvious attempt to find a more comfortable position. "Were you worried about me then? Good to know."

"Shouldn't you be resting?" Akash changed the subject abruptly and not quite as smoothly as he'd hoped. "In bed?"

"Want to help me get undressed?" Hamish's voice deepened only slightly, but the change went straight through Akash as though the man had reached out to grab him by the cock. "Akash? You all right? Are you blushing? Why on earth would you be blushing? Something you'd like to tell me?"

"I'll just clean up the dishes." Akash stood to make a quick escape, only for strong fingers to wrap around his wrist to stop him midstep. He glanced down at the tanned, calloused, and scarred hand instead of trying to meet the intense blue eyes watching him. "Or, I can wash up after we get you into bed."

Hamish ran his fingers firmly around Akash's wrist. They stroked along the palm of his hand, paying careful attention to the various burn scars. "Baking battle wounds?"

"Every baker worth his salt has them." Akash forced his breath out, all his years of martial arts training coming in handy to keep himself under control. He never imagined a simple touch along his wrist or hand could evoke such a forceful sexual energy. "I've no doubts you have your own scars."

"I do." Hamish pulled on his wrist until Akash sat beside him again. He guided their hands underneath his shirt until Akash's fingers touched the marred skin along his side. "Knife wound."

"From?"

"Classified." Hamish winked at him with an uncharacteristically mischievous twinkle in his eyes. "Why don't you help me get ready for bed? I'll show you all the other scars."

Akash didn't know if even his twenty-plus years of training could help him maintain his cool façade. "Aren't you supposed to be skilled enough to avoid injury?"

"The mouse isn't my first misstep—I doubt it'll be my last." Hamish's almost predatory smile morphed into a more serious one. "No warrior emerges from the shadows without damage in one form or another."

Akash found his fingers being guided across the scars mapped across Hamish's muscled chest and stomach. He closed his eyes to allow touch to evoke an image, instead of his vision. "One day you'll have to share your stories with me."

"One day?"

He eased his hand firmly out of Hamish's grasp. "Yes, not today when I can clearly see you wince with every movement. Are you always such a stubborn moron?"

"Frequently."

"Up you get then." Akash waited for Hamish to stand before getting up himself. "You've had a day of travel. Will you want a shower?"

"A bath," Hamish corrected. "You could always help me wash my back."

Do not get turned on.

Do not think about Hamish naked in the bath.

Do not think about washing more than his sodding back.

I bet he's got scars on more than his chest—and those hairs I could feel. I'm sure those cover his thighs, and now my cock's harder than a rolling pin.

Shit.

"Akash? You all right?" Hamish waved his uninjured hand in front of his face. "You've stopped in the middle of the hall. Something wrong?"

"What? No. Nothing. I'm fine. It's fine. Everything is brilliant." Akash rambled like his little sister did when caught disobeying. "What were you saying?"

Hamish smiled tiredly at him. "If I didn't feel as if I'd been trampled into the ground, I'd be incredibly interested in what caused your trousers to appear so tight."

"Arse."

Taking matters into his own hand, Akash bullied Hamish down the hall toward his bedroom. The man had the nerve to chuckle when they went the wrong direction. *Honestly. He could've helped me out a bit. It's his flat.* They found the right door with the injured man still laughing.

It took a bit of careful work to get Hamish out of his shirt and sling. Akash helped him with his boots and socks before starting to step away to allow the man privacy. Those same fingers grabbed his wrist again to stop him.

"Aren't you going to help me with my trousers as well?" Hamish stared intently at him, not even a hint of a smile on his face. "I've nothing to hide."

Well, I'm going to have something to bloody hide if I have to come face-to-cock with your naked body.

No amount of meditation prepared him for peeling off Hamish's jeans and boxers. Akash sternly focused all of his energy on not staring at the perfection bouncing inches from his nose. It had been a while since he'd spent time inspecting another man's cock.

Living at home for so long, Akash hadn't dated much. He'd had a few boyfriends. None he'd ever considered bringing to meet his parents.

"Making a study of me?" Hamish reached a hand down to run his fingers through Akash's hair. He dropped his arm a moment later with a groan. *"Fuck."*

With one last lingering gaze at the masculine beauty in front of him, Akash stood back up. He went and filled the bath with hot water, then bustled Hamish into it. The bulk of man sunk into the large tub with a heavy sigh.

"A sponge bath seems more Freddie's line of work than mine." Akash held a bar of soap uncertainly in his hand. *Where does one start to wash the body of a man they've only kissed? No, Akash, not his dick.* "Can you lean forward a bit?"

Hamish blinked at a few times before reaching for the soap. "Maybe I should do it."

"Oh? How?" Akash lifted the soap out of reach. "Stubbornness to the point of hurting yourself further is idiotic."

After a slightly clumsy beginning where the soap bar insisted on shooting out of his hand multiple times, Akash gently washed every glorious inch of Hamish's body. He winced at the hiss of pain when his fingers strayed over the bruised and swollen injured shoulder. As he moved on to his chest, Hamish rested against the side of the tub and closed his eyes.

Exploring at his own pace, Akash traced every scar on the sun-bronzed skin. The tattoos didn't necessarily shock him. He'd yet to meet a marine without at least one to commemorate their military service.

The Royal Marine badge on his chest was standard tattoo fare. The massive ink covering Hamish's entire back had surprised him. Between his shoulders sat a black-and-white Victoria Cross; underneath it at least twenty names had been etched in his flesh.

"That's a lot of names." Akash found himself desperate for conversation, to avoid thinking too deeply over where his fingers currently rested. *Bloody hell, his thighs are massive and strong.* "Soldiers you knew?"

"Marines." Hamish watched him through half-open eyes. "Men I knew who lost their lives in Afghanistan."

"Did you receive a Victoria Cross?" Akash wondered if the medal meant more than a symbol representing lost souls. "Or is it only for them?"

"Both." Hamish shifted in the water, sloshing some of it

over the side. "They said I was brave in the face of the enemy."

"And?"

"I came home." Hamish jerked his head toward the names tattooed on his back. "They trusted me and my decisions. They came home in caskets."

Akash froze with his hand by a scarred knee, and his fingers clutched the bar of soap tightly. Pain filtered through each word Hamish spoke. "They live through you—through the names on your back."

"Yes."

No words could make the palpable pain disappear. Akash didn't even bother making an attempt. He turned his attention instead to offering comfort in the form of a wash in the warm, sudsy water.

Akash rested his hand flat on Hamish's lower back when he leaned forward slightly; his fingers splayed across the list of fallen marines. "You've done them proud. I've no doubts in my mind."

"I hope so."

CHAPTER FIFTEEN

HAMISH

Ross men never bared their souls to anyone. His father had evoked all the staid nonsense of stiff upper lips. He'd been a kind and good man, but he'd never shown his son how to handle a wealth and depth of emotions.

Grieving, as a result, hadn't come naturally to Hamish. Whether his parents' deaths or the loss of marines in his command, he felt each one keenly but eventually dismissed it. His tattoos had become a way to say what he found to be impossible to voice.

We carry on, son.

So he did.

And had done.

"Whatever you've got going through your mind, it can't

be good for you. Your face will stick in that frown if you're not careful." Akash had finished helping him to dry off, and moved on to hunting through Hamish's wardrobe. "Where are your pants? Or do you sleep starkers?"

All things considered, Hamish thought he'd been the picture of restraint throughout the evening. A man he found intoxicatingly attractive had given him a wash in the bath. He hadn't once attempted to drag him into the water for a kiss.

Not once.

All that damned willpower hasn't gone to waste.

But bloody hell, I want a taste of his lips—and everything else.

"Not entirely certain I care to know what you're thinking about now, but at least it's stopped you frowning so fiercely." Akash stood by the wardrobe with a pair of Hamish's boxers dangling from his hand. His eyes drifted down to the visibly growing erection. "No naughty thoughts. The doctor wouldn't approve."

"Sod the doctor." Hamish strode across the room. He might not be able to lift his arms up, but had no doubts he could work around the issue. "Take your clothes off."

"That an order?" Akash lifted an eyebrow while his eyes seemed to sparkle with a dark amusement. "Is this what happens to you military types? You forget how to behave out of uniform?"

"*Take* your clothes off." Hamish crowded into the baker's space. He'd skirted around the issue for long enough. *Shoulder be damned—I'll see every inch of his skin tonight.* "Well? Get on with it."

With a wry smile, Akash carelessly kicked off one trainer, then the other. He toed his socks off next. Hamish laughed at the absurdly lengthy process the man went through to ease out of his shirt, trousers, and briefs.

"Make a meal of it, why don't you." Hamish backed Akash up until he dropped onto the bed, which filled almost 70 percent of the room. "How about I make a meal out of you?"

Akash scooted up on the bed until he rested against the headboard. His breathing picked up while he watched Hamish. "Sure you can manage with your shoulder?"

Hamish stalked around to stand next to the reclining baker. He caught him by the hair with his good hand. "Do you consent?"

"To what?"

"Everything."

"Gladly." Akash grinned a little wildly up at him. "*Willingly.*"

Hamish yanked him forward by his hair, ignoring the slight twitch in his shoulder. He rubbed his thick erection across Akash's lips. "Are you certain?"

"Ye—"

Nudging his way into the open mouth, Hamish cut Akash off midanswer. He smiled down into the eyes glaring up at him. A jolt of lust and joy raced up his spine; maybe just this once, he'd met someone who could be everything he craved and more.

The stubble on Akash's jaw grazed against his skin, drawing his attention back to the lips wrapped tightly around his erection. Hamish tightened his fingers around the thick, soft raven locks. He tugged hard enough to delve deeper into the warmth of his inviting mouth.

"Stroke yourself." Hamish tapped a finger against Akash's forehead to get his attention. "You'll come when I do."

A tilt of the baker's eyebrows conveyed his amusement at being ordered about. Hamish shifted his hand to the back of Akash's head. He managed, without tweaking his shoulder too much, to control the speed and depth of the mouth gliding up and down on his shaft.

"Enjoying yourself as much as I am?" Hamish couldn't help the cruel tease, since Akash had no way to respond to him aside from a narrowing of his eyes. "Nice and slowly, slide your fingers up and down. Don't want you finishing before I do."

The teasing encouragement apparently struck Akash as a challenge. In no time at all, he demonstrated to Hamish a wickedly skilled talent with his tongue. He etched away at Hamish's sanity with every flick, hum, and inhale.

Locking his knees to avoid dropping to them, Hamish tried desperately to regain some semblance of control. He used his hold on Akash's hair to slow him down. It only served to allow him more time to utilise his tongue, swirling it around the head of Hamish's cock.

If I fall and dislocate my shoulder again, it's definitely going to be worth it.

Fuck.

He didn't fall. Or, dislocate his shoulder, again. Akash ended up with his chest covered in the evidence of their mutual pleasure.

Hamish sank down on the floor beside him, and grunted when it jolted his injury. "I'd offer to help you in the bath, but I'm fairly sure you've done me in."

Akash glanced down at the mess on his chest. "I'll be back in a moment."

Hamish struggled up to his feet and carefully stretched out on top of the duvet on his bed with a satisfied sigh. "He's brilliant."

So I better not bugger it all up.

The strain of being in pain all day wore on Hamish. He wiggled around to get himself into a more comfortable position on the bed. His eyes closed as he sank into the afterglow of the first shared sexual pleasure he'd had in a while.

I'm keeping him.

Definitely.

"You're far too pleased with yourself." Akash's laugh brought him out of a light doze. "Should I swan off home then?"

No.

Hamish lazily waved him over. He had no intention of allowing Akash to blow and go. "Stay."

CHAPTER SIXTEEN

AKASH

Shanti: Aki? Are you there? I've been trying to call you for ten minutes. Nye said you stayed over at Hamish's place. Why aren't you answering your phone?

Akash: What are you doing up at one in the morning? What's wrong?

Shanti: Nye was taking me home from the Sin Bin when we saw smoke coming out of the bakery. I've called 999.

"Fuck."

"Akash?" Hamish reached out to turn on a light, only to drop back with a groan. "Bloody arm."

"I hope it's not bloody." Akash sat up and fumbled with the lamp on the nightstand. "Shanti texted me; my bakery is on fire. I've got to go."

"Fire? What?" Hamish shot up out of bed, pushing through the pain. "I'll come with."

"You sure?" Akash dressed more quickly than he could ever remember doing. He fought down his impatience while helping Hamish with his jeans. "Let's go."

He'd gotten them both fully clothed before a terrifying thought occurred to him. *Ganesh. My cat. I have a cat. Fuck.* He fumbled with his phone to give his sister a call. Nye answered instead and calmly explained he'd managed to get safely into the flat to retrieve the cat when Shanti had tried to do it herself.

I suppose I'll have to be nice to him now.

They talked briefly. Nye hung up once the fire brigade arrived. He promised to keep Shanti, and the cat, away from danger.

Hamish grabbed his keys from the table in the living room. "Take mine."

"Fine." Akash didn't care who drove what as long as they made it to the bakery before his life savings went up in ashes. "What am I going to do?"

Hamish covered his hand that rested on the steering wheel. "First, take a few deep breaths. Second, remember you are not alone in this world; you've family and friends who are here to help you rebuild whatever the damage might be. Third, if you wreck my vehicle because you're panicked, I might have to take you over my knees and give you a good spanking."

Akash glanced at the hand covering his, and then over to the man attached to it. "Bare arse and all?"

"Let's not get distracted." Hamish squeezed his hand

before easing back into the seat. "I've a friend who works with the fire brigade. I'll give him a call while you drive."

While Hamish chatted with his friend, Akash focused all his attention on not wrecking the car. His heart sank into his stomach when billowing smoke could be seen as he turned the corner. He parked down the street to avoid blocking the emergency crew.

Shanti and Nye were waiting for them when they got out of the Mercedes. His little sister rushed over to him to throw one arm around his waist while her other clutched a hissing Ganesh. Akash stared over her head to what had once been his bakery.

The fire appeared to have burned hot and seemed mostly centred in the front of the bakery. *Please let it be so.* Water from the fire brigade had clearly done its job. What the flames hadn't ruined, the dampness likely would.

"How the bloody hell did this happen?" Akash couldn't understand how his dream bakery had vanished in a roaring fire. He always checked everything before shutting down at night. "It's all gone."

"Oh, Aki. I'm so sorry." Shanti squeezed her arms around him with Ganesh squashed between them; her tears dampened his T-shirt. "We'll help you put it all back together."

"This isn't a vase you can fix with glue." Akash gently eased her out of the embrace and over toward Nye. "Take her home, will you? I'll call around once I have answers. Can you keep Ganesh with you?"

Shanti often cat-sat Ganesh for him. Akash didn't have the mental energy to worry about it for now. His cat would be safe and spoiled rotten by his little sister.

"Of course, but I should—"

When Shanti started to argue, Nye shook his head at her. Akash loved his sister dearly, but he couldn't handle tears right now. He had to assess the damage without his emotions tripping him up.

I'll sob my eyes out in a pillow after I know if my dream's gone.

After the smoke had cleared and the danger passed, Akash still wasn't allowed into the building. The words arson investigation floated right over his head. He could only stare at the bakery with the dawning realisation that everything he owned had likely gone up in smoke as well.

They waited.

And waited.

And waited.

Hamish looped his arm around Akash's shoulders to hold him close. "The upstairs doesn't appear too badly damaged. I imagine they'll let you in if it's safe, to get clothes and such."

Akash rubbed his eyes. "They're not going to let me live here, are they."

"Probably not until the investigation is over—and they've determined the structure is sound." Hamish dropped his arm after a moment. "Sodding shoulder. You can stay with me. I've got plenty of space and even a spare room if you're worried about it seeming *too soon*, or whatever nonsense you come up with."

Before Akash began to formulate his argument, one of the firefighters peeled away from the others to join them.

Hamish had been right in his assessment. The second floor flat had suffered smoke damage, but the flames hadn't directly affected it.

The firefighter, who insisted on being called Lennie, provided an escort into the bakery. The man tried to explain about the investigation, but Akash didn't hear a word of it. His mind wouldn't process anything other than the blackened remnants of his shop.

They carefully picked their way around the damaged areas to the stairs in the back, which were completely untouched. Akash breathed a sigh of relief when he discovered all of his belongings untouched by fire. They might require a thorough air out and clean, but his clothes, computer, and everything else remained intact.

Quickly throwing a bag of essentials together, Akash packed enough clothes to ensure he wouldn't have to come back for a week or more. He had no idea how many days or months an investigation might take. His worries were slightly put at ease by Lennie assuring him the entire property would be secured to prevent theft.

Not that I've anything left worth stealing.

Picking up his small stash of emergency cash, Akash also retrieved his laptop and toiletries. He made a mental note to contact his insurance company. They'd hopefully cover the entire cost of rebuilding; he had no intention of going backwards and returning to the bakery in Fowey.

Akash stood forlornly on the pavement outside of his shop; his mood plummeted in the acrid smoke still hovering in the air. He tasted it with each breath. "What a sodding nightmare."

Life had only just begun to come together for him. Two bakeries. He had a flat of his own. A dashing man had barged into his world with no desire to leave. Everything had looked to be going brilliantly.

Akash lost his grip on his bags, and his knees went out from under him, as well. He dropped to the kerb with a bruising thud. "I can't. What the bloody hell am I going to do now? Fuck. My parents. They'll be devastated."

I'm devastated.

Hamish crouched in front of him to lay a hand on Akash's knee. "Why don't we get you home? I've already talked to my friend who works as an arson investigator. I called the office as well. We'll have someone out here to keep an eye on the bakery to keep anyone from getting into it who isn't allowed."

Akash lifted up his hand to show how violently it trembled. "You can't drive, and I'm not sure I should."

"You've had a shock." Hamish glanced around until he spotted someone. "Oi. Lennie. Get your arse over here."

Akash watched the handsome black firefighter jog over toward them. "You know him?"

"Not well. I know his husband. We served together." Hamish stood up to greet Lennie with a hand held out. "Haven't seen you in ages. Spoke to Marc, he thinks they'll call him out to investigate."

"You know I can't say anything." Lennie's gaze shifted over to Akash. "You're a bit peaky. Why haven't you taken him home, Hamish?"

Hamish gestured toward the sling. "I'd rather not risk it."

"Ah." Lennie scratched his head for a moment before

wiping away the sweat and grime on his forehead. "Tell you what, I'll see if they can spare me for a minute to drive you and have Marc to meet us at your flat so he can give me a lift back. One catastrophe is enough for one day. We don't want you getting into an accident. You might have to wait a bit."

The next hour went by in a blur for Akash. They bundled him into the back of the vehicle. Lennie didn't bother with conversation, only turned on the radio and drove them straight to Hamish's flat.

"Keep an eye on him. Think he'll be fine. A cup of tea and something sugary might help," Lennie muttered in an aside to Hamish, though Akash could hear them both clearly. "What happened to your shoulder?"

"Tripped."

"Tripped? I sense a story. How about you and your baker come over to supper later in the week?" Lennie invited. He glanced over at Akash in the back seat. "I'd say it was great to meet you, but the circumstances leave something to be desired. The chief'll let you know when it's safe to return. We'll send you a report as well. You might want to contact your insurance."

Akash nodded. He hadn't heard a word, not a single one. All he wanted to do was to sink into the blissful ignorance of sleep and forget the last few hours for a bit.

"I'd tell you it'll look better in the morning, but you'll feel worse, I imagine." Lennie turned away when a horn sounded. "There's my Marc. See you, lads, later."

Akash stumbled out of the Mercedes right into Hamish, who wrapped his good arm around him tightly. "Sorry."

"Want tea?"

"Not particularly." Akash didn't believe in tea solving a multitude of problems. "Unless you plan on spiking it with something stronger."

"We'll see what I can find." Hamish must've been exhausted, but the man never showed it. Akash had to admire his stoic ability to soldier through the pain of a dislocated shoulder. "Want a hand with your bags?"

Shaking his head, Akash trudged behind Hamish into his flat with his bags. He dropped them just inside the door, and fell face first onto the sofa with a dramatic groan. In the morning, he would attempt to find perspective, but for now, he intended to have a good moan about the situation.

Even if I'm only whinging to myself.

What the hell am I going to do?

Akash sat up on the couch, leaning forward with his face buried in his hands. He dragged his fingers roughly through his hair with a muttered curse when Hamish held out a mug to him. "I don't want any sodding tea."

"Good. It's the strongest whisky I own." Hamish waved the cup in front of him. "Have a few sips and budge over so I can sit next to you."

"Is this supposed to help?"

"Old marine fable—whisky and a friend cure most problems."

"You made that shit up." Akash glared suspiciously but took the drink and shifted down on the sofa.

"If it works, does it matter?" Hamish eased down on the cushions with a groan. "Sodding shoulder. You can console yourself that you don't have the ignominy of tripping over a mouse."

Akash offered him the mug. "You might need this more than me."

CHAPTER SEVENTEEN

HAMISH

The morning after the fire, Hamish sat for an hour watching Akash sleep. He imagined neither of them had slept restfully. His shoulder had kept him from doing more than dozing.

He ignored his first instinct to plan a way to help Akash; it seemed wiser to wait things out. Hamish didn't believe the baker would take kindly to him bulldozing over him. He wouldn't have in his position.

His mother had always told him to treat others the way he wanted to be treated. *If you hate something, love, why would you do it to anyone else?* Hamish missed her—missed both of his parents. She would've adored Akash; his father might've required more convincing.

"Wasn't a dream, was it?" Akash asked groggily.

Ah, denial, the easiest of the stages of grief to sort out.

"Not a dream. Not even a nightmare." Hamish refused to sugar-coat things for him. "Ready to face the day?"

"Not even fucking close." Akash dragged the pillow over his face and screamed into it for a few seconds. He tossed it toward the end of the bed. "Not much choice, is there?"

"No." Hamish dropped his hand onto Akash's arm. "Why don't we go out for coffee? We can stop by to see what the damage is."

Nodding absently, Akash bent over the edge of the bed to fumble around in his trousers. He sat back up with his mobile in hand. Hamish headed into the bathroom to allow him some semblance of privacy while he spoke with his parents.

Getting his T-shirt off required a great deal of dexterity and pain, but Hamish finally managed it. He twisted around in front of the mirror to get a better view of the bruising and swelling. His shoulder had coloured up rather impressively; he supposed, like everything else in life, it could've been much worse.

I've had worse.

With doctor's orders to take it easy for a few weeks, Hamish had intended to stick to his desk. He wondered absently if perhaps he might spend the time with Akash, instead. His assistance might be in spirit only given his physical limitations, but it would at least be more than nothing.

"Hamish?" Akash tentatively knocked on the bathroom door. "The insurance company should be sending someone around to check out the bakery. Your friend Lennie texted me to say they've turned over the investigation to detectives. I'm going to need a lot of coffee to deal with this shit."

"Be out in a moment." Hamish finished checking on his injury. He hoped the pain faded sooner rather than later. "There's an en suite in the spare room if you want to get ready instead of waiting for me."

By the time they'd both gotten ready, Hamish had text messages of his own from Lennie and his husband, Marc. Neither of them could divulge anything concrete about the fire. They wouldn't risk the investigation; knowing detectives had gotten involved spoke volumes in and of itself.

His gut instinct told him the fire hadn't been an accident. Hamish even had a suspicion on who might be responsible, either directly or indirectly. He'd wait to see what the *official* investigation came up with before he stuck himself into it.

"Hamish?"

He glanced over at the door and realised he'd gotten lost in thought. "I'm done, I'm done."

"Sure you don't want a hand?"

"I'll give you a hand." Hamish stepped out of the bathroom to find a fully dressed Akash sitting on the edge of the bed. "How are your parents?"

"Devastated for me." Akash hopped up to give him a hand in getting his shirt over his head. "They wanted to drive out to help me clean the place up. I put them off. I've no idea when the investigators will let me start or how much insurance will cover. If I didn't love the area so much, I'd consider cutting my losses and moving the shop."

"Did you contact the twins?" Hamish tried to subtly guide the conversation to see where Akash's thoughts might be.

"Don't they usually work in the mornings?"

"They think their father did it." Akash eyed him for a second before continuing. "You agree."

"I do."

"Should you be resting?" Akash waited until they'd gotten situated in the vehicle to ask. He'd insisted on driving, since Hamish had no doubt his ability to function would be best kept for emergencies only. "Not sure 'take it easy' really translates to swanning around Cardiff with me."

Hamish gingerly shifted in the seat to reach over and adjust the back of it to a slightly reclined position. "See? I'm resting."

With an exaggerated roll of his eyes, Akash apparently decided it was time to go. He pulled out of the parking space and barely managed to avoid the wrought iron gate. Hamish chuckled at the sheepish grin aimed in his direction.

"Let's try to get there in one piece, shall we?" Hamish met Akash's glare with a blank stare. "Might want to look both ways."

"Thanks."

"Happy to help." Hamish reached into his pocket when his mobile buzzed, to find a text from Nye.

Nye: The cat has so far scratched up my sofa, relieved himself in my closet, and hacked up a hairball on the floor.

Hamish: Maybe he wants you to feel special.

Nye: The blasted furball ruined my favourite jacket.

Hamish: I weep for you.

Nye: Fucking cat.

Hamish: You could always tell Shanti to stay at her own

place instead of yours.

Nye: I'm prepared to suffer.

"Do I want to know why you're chuckling like some evil henchman in a cartoon?" Akash broke into his thoughts. "You haven't said a word for ages."

Hamish lifted his eyes from his mobile to find Akash watching him intently. He glanced around in surprise to discover they'd already arrived at Stag Coffee, one of his favourite breakfast places in the city. "Nye's having a bit of trouble with your cat."

"Ah."

Hamish tilted the screen to show a video Nye had sent of Ganesh racing around his flat full tilt. "He's apparently making a lifelong friend."

"Maybe it'll keep him out of my sister's pants." Akash brightened for the first time since the fire while watching the video.

"Doubtful."

Akash waved his hand as if to bat away the word. "I don't mind, actually. Shanti's strong enough to make her own choices. Nye's a good man. I'll still break his good leg if he hurts her."

"I've a feeling she'd do it herself." Hamish admired the way the youngest member of the Robinson family had stood up to the rest without backing down. "How about breakfast? I've a sudden craving for their full breakfast. I'm buying."

"Good. I might be destitute by the time this is all over." Akash's laugh sounded slightly hysterical. "God. This is happening, isn't it?"

Hamish took him by the chin to force their eyes to meet. "It is, so keep calm and get ready to kick arse—even if it's your own to get it in gear."

"Pretty sure that's not how the quote goes." Akash hopped out of the vehicle and waited for Hamish to join him.

"Like mine better." Hamish grabbed him by the shoulder to lead him toward the café. "Carry on is *too* mild."

CHAPTER EIGHTEEN

AKASH

The week dripped by like slow torture. Akash went from angry to dazed to depressed in a dizzying cycle of emotions. His only relief came from Hamish, who offered comfortable, silent support.

Their close quarters brought none of the awkwardness Akash feared. His younger sister teased him about moving in with his lover before they'd done anything. He'd no intention of correcting her; some knowledge shouldn't be shared with siblings.

We'll both be scarred for life.

He'd met with Marc Maddox, Lennie's husband and the man in charge of the arson investigation. The bakery would be released to him in a few days. They'd completed the evidence gathering part of the inquiry.

His insurance agreed to cover the clean-up and repairs. Akash intended to do the majority of the clearing out himself. Not only would it save money, but he'd work out some of his rage at how callous the arsonist had been.

Alice and Alex had avoided him for most of the week. Guilt overwhelmed them. Akash knew they needed time to process; none of them needed an investigation to tell them the twins' father had a hand in setting the fire. It seemed right up his alley.

"So, when are you going to introduce me to one of these rugby men, eh?" Jack had driven out from Fowey with his massive Irish wolfhound, Stevie. They'd driven out to Heath Park to give the exuberant creature a walk. "I'm languishing in the village with no one for company but Vi, who's always mooning after her beau."

"Languishing?" Akash gave the dramatic barber a roll of his eyes in response. "You had two dates last week."

"Bad ones." Jack took a stick Stevie brought to him and threw it far out across the grassy field. "I'm bored in Fowey."

A bored Jack was a dangerous one.

"Why don't you move shop? You could be a barber anywhere." Akash had listened to his friend talk about leaving Fowey for years, but he'd never actually made an attempt at it. "Or take a vacation. Do something."

"Do something other than moan?" Jack went silent briefly while continuing the game of fetch with his hound. "How about you? What will you do with the bakery?"

"Rebuild," Akash answered confidently. "How are you

with a hammer?"

"Terrible. When do you need me to be there? I've got time off built up at the barbershop." Jack called Stevie back to them so they could continue down the path. "Think you'll be open before December?"

"I hope so." Akash might not celebrate Christmas, but he did a massive amount of business during the holiday season. "We'll see how the insurance company handles things once I get all the damage cleaned out."

"And how's your marine?"

"He's not mine." Akash grabbed a stray branch to pick the bark off as a distraction. He'd worked hard in the last few days *not* to put any pressure on himself or Hamish. They might temporarily live together, but it didn't mean their growing connection should be rushed by them or their well-meaning friends. "He's good, though."

Jack pivoted on his heel and shifted over to stop in front of Akash. "There isn't one set pace for a relationship to move. You know this, right? Go as fast or as slow as you want. I'd wager my salary for the month that Freddie and Graham have had this exact discussion with you."

"*Jack.*" Akash didn't care to listen to a third version of the conversation. "Perpetual bachelors shouldn't throw stones into other people's ponds."

"Think your phrase got lost in translation." Jack wrinkled his nose at him. "All I'll say is, don't sabotage a good thing."

"You must be confusing me for Graham."

Of their group of friends, Graham had, up until recently, been the one with deep-rooted commitment issues. Akash exchanged a bemused grin with Jack when they thought about the redheaded wanderer now shacked up with BC. They still found the changes in their old friend entertaining.

"Akash?"

"Hmm?" He dodged the puddle in the path and glanced over at Jack. "What?"

"I know you've got the whole mystical Zen shit going for you, but it's all right to be hacked off someone tried to burn your place to the ground." Jack held up a hand to stop him from arguing. "You've never done angry."

"Mystical Zen shit? Really? What's the point of losing my mind now?" Akash might know exactly where to lay the blame for the fire, but running off for revenge wouldn't help anyone. "I'm not going to throw a tantrum."

"Good. I'd shove you in the mud." Jack hooked Stevie up to his leash and ended up being half-dragged down the path. "Bloody dog. Are you coming?"

"Better view from back here." Akash used his mobile to get blackmail footage of the idiot being dragged along by his giant of a dog. "Stop if you hit the sea."

"Arse." Jack managed to get Stevie under control. His eyes narrowed when he spotted the phone pointed in his direction. "Are you taping me?"

"Not at this precise moment."

"Arse."

CHAPTER NINETEEN

HAMISH

As Akash intended to spend the day with a friend, Hamish opted to grab a cab to the office. Staying in his flat doing nothing didn't sit well with him at all; better to get work done. Even with physical therapy, he figured it would be another week before he could drive without risking a crash.

He'd left his apartment before the sun came up and while Akash still slept. They'd been cooped up together for a week, and the easy way they'd found a daily routine probably should've concerned him. It didn't.

The annoying voice in the back of his mind told him it might be a sign of how good they could be as a couple. Hamish refused to think on it while Akash floundered in an emotionally vulnerable state. When things with the bakery settled and his shoulder had healed, he'd ask him out for a date and another and another.

Then we'll see. I'm not rushing into anything.

"Are you supposed to be at work?" Wyatt stuck his head into Hamish's office at seven in the morning. "Didn't the docs tell you to take it easy?"

"I've done nothing for a week." Hamish gestured toward several of the stacks of paper on his desk. "This strains my mind, not my muscles."

"Doc clear you for coffee?" Wyatt dropped into the chair across from Hamish and stretched his long legs out.

"As if I'd stop drinking coffee because a doctor fucking told me to." Hamish would go to his grave with a mug of the stuff clutched tightly in his hand. "You buying?"

"Me?" Wyatt leant forward to get a closer glance at one of the invoices. "Did they actually invoice every single thing they ate?"

"Jokers, the lot of them." Hamish had made the mistake of lecturing everyone in the office on not itemising their expense reports while travelling. He now had lines and lines of overly detailed statements by way of revenge. "I'm regretting my decision to try to work today."

"Where's your British stiff upper lip?"

Hamish grabbed a pen and flung it at Wyatt, who batted it away. "Was there a purpose to your visit?"

"Coffee."

"Love some."

Coffee did nothing to improve Hamish's disinterest in the tedious part of his job. He forced himself through three quarters of the stacks before throwing in the towel. The files weren't going anywhere. As long as bills and salaries got paid, the rest could wait.

Before Hamish had time to search for a distraction, one arrived in the form of two pale, blond teenagers. Alice and Alex fidgeted awkwardly for a few minutes before shuffling into his office with a bemused Wyatt behind them. He promised to bring "weird British tea shit" and left the three of them alone in the room.

"We haven't seen you two in a few days. You all right?" Hamish prompted after a prolonged silence where it became apparent the two wouldn't speak first. "Did you need help?"

"Can you kill someone?"

"*Alex*," Alice interrupted her brother sharply. "We don't want to kill anyone."

Alex slumped into his chair with a glare at his twin. "Maybe."

Hamish waited for them to settle down. "We don't usually assassinate people."

"Probably get paid better if we did." Wyatt returned, causing both of the twins to jump. He set the tray down on the table and took a seat when Hamish waved him toward one. "Can you pay?"

"*Earp.*" Hamish knew from his conversations with Akash that the twins often struggled to know when someone was teasing them. He didn't want them getting the wrong idea. "We absolutely do not assassinate people; I doubt that's what you're looking for either. How can I help?"

The two exchanged glances, nudging one another. Hamish

decided it was best to allow them to tell it in their own time. He made a sharp gesture to Wyatt to ensure he didn't try prodding them to speak; it would only serve to discourage rather than encourage.

It took almost thirty minutes for the twins to explain in what they believed to be a detailed manner what they wanted. They appeared convinced the arson investigation wouldn't find anything. Their concern had caused a massive amount of anxiety of their belief that their stepdad would get away with hiring a friend to set the blaze.

They had no proof.

Hamish tried to assure them if their stepdad had been responsible, then he would be punished for it. The look they sent him spoke of a lengthy history of similar assurances eventually coming to nothing. In the end, he promised to do anything in his power to help.

They slurped their tea quickly, and raced out of the office like the hounds of hell were on their heels. Wyatt's eyes flicked from the now empty chairs over to Hamish. He lifted his eyebrows with an obvious question.

"We're not shooting him." Hamish refused to admit how tempting it was, given what he knew about the man. "I'll give Marc a call to see how the investigation is going."

"Because they asked?"

Hamish swirled the small amount of tea left in his cup, watching a chunk of biscuit going around in a circle. "Do you have any idea how much courage it took two autistics to walk into a place they've never been and ask me for help?"

"A great deal, I'm sure, but we're still not private

investigators or *Miami Vice*." Wyatt grabbed one of the leftover biscuits and tossed it into his mouth. "Seriously, Hamster, what's the point?"

Hamish rubbed his forehead and prayed for strength. "The point, you irritating Yankee arsehole, is they're scared, and if I can help, I will."

"Good." Wyatt snagged another cookie with a grin. "If they want work while the bakery is out of commission, send them over to Aled. He could use a few extra hands in his garden. He's good at being quiet."

"I'll never understand why he chose to marry you." Hamish dodged the chunk of biscuit thrown at him. "Will you quit throwing shit at my head? My office is littered with all the crap you fling at me constantly."

CHAPTER TWENTY

AKASH

Standing in the middle of his wrecked bakery, Akash tried to squash his emotions into a tiny space in his heart. One reason he'd decided to get a first look at it on his own was he didn't want to break down in front of anyone. When Lennie contacted him to let him know they were releasing it to him, he'd driven straight to his shop.

To his immense disbelief, almost all the damage appeared to be cosmetic instead of structural. He dropped to his knees, oblivious to the broken glass and splintered wooden flooring digging into his legs. Relief brought tears to his eyes; he tilted his head to stare up at the ceiling blackened by smoke.

I can do this.

I can.

It's not as bad as I thought.

Why am I sobbing on the floor of my bakery like a toddler?

"Oi. You all right?"

How much fucking bad karma do I have built up?

Akash slowly got to his feet, carefully brushing the broken glass off his jeans. "Scottie."

"I know I'm an arse."

Akash couldn't help a loud snort of amusement. "Understatement of the year, but continue."

Scottie rubbed the back of his neck and stared over at the rubble where counters had once stood. "Can I help with getting rid of this debris? Got a mate who works in waste management, he's promised to bring a few of his largest skip bags out for you. Fill 'em up, he'll haul them away."

"Free of charge?"

"Look, you want the help or not?" Scottie shrugged. "I can fuck off back to bed and sleep for the rest of the day."

"How kind of you." Akash lifted his hand up to stop Scottie from responding. "I'd appreciate the help—the attitude I can live without."

"Picky little shit, aren't you?"

"If you've ever wondered why you're single, it's because you're an areshole." Akash watched the idiot carefully. He might be there to offer assistance, but he'd proved himself to be dangerously impulsive at the best of times.

"Is it? I thought I'd scared them off with my massive cock." Scottie grabbed his crotch as if to demonstrate. "Sure I can't tempt you?"

"I'd rather hump a porcupine." Akash would honestly

rather have rolled around naked on glass and rusted nails. "If you're here to help, then do something useful. If you're here to badger me for a date, fuck off and find someone who's actually interested."

"Tetchy, tetchy."

In his years of experience in dealing with men like Scottie, Akash knew the wisest decision was to ignore him. He focused instead on texting friends and family on the state of the bakery. Several promised almost immediately to bring over cleaning supplies. He wanted to vent his emotions in private, but rebuilding required more than his own hands.

All the broken windows had been sealed off with boards by the fire brigade for security. Akash made a call to order new glass to be delivered. He sent an email to his insurance to see if they'd approved the renovations and contractor he intended to hire once everything had been cleared out.

With the money from insurance and some of his savings, Akash planned to make a few improvements to the shop, and more importantly to the kitchen. *More ovens, better ones, and more space.* Turning a potential disaster into a positive mattered to him. Whatever the intentions of the person who set fire to the bakery, he refused to allow them to succeed.

Hamish: We've nothing planned at the office today. Got room in this clean up for a bunch of military twits? We'll bring beer and pizza. Wyatt swears you can't have a 'pick crap up party' without both.

Akash: Make sure he doesn't put any weird shit on the pizza.

Hamish: Need anything else?

Akash: Patience and paracetamol. Scottie decided to show up to help.

Hamish: Is he actually helping or is it his deluded concept of it?

Akash: Undetermined.

Hamish: We'll hurry and bring extra beer.

Akash: Maybe less. It is Scottie.

The skip bags arrived, with his reinforcements following not long after. Scottie had called in his rugby mates turned business partners. Akash couldn't recall his shop ever being quite so jam-packed with testosterone—ever.

Alice and Alex showed up, only for the latter to immediately suffer a shutdown. Wyatt, of all people, offered to take them over to his place. His husband's low-key personality and their quiet garden suited the young autistics better than a crowded and noisy construction zone filled with large men with bigger egos.

For three days, the ragtag group of friends worked to scrub every smoke-damaged surface. Ruined shelves were ripped out. Anything the fire touched went into the rubbish heap. Akash said farewell to all of his beloved equipment. Even knowing the replacements would be superior didn't diminish his momentary sadness; they'd been his first purchases in his own shop.

Well, maybe not my first, but the first I claimed on my own that my mum hadn't touched first.

By the fourth day, Akash lost all of his helpers except for Hamish, Shanti, and Nye. The latter joked that between Hamish and himself they had one fully functioning man.

Shanti informed all of them they were equally useless; she wisely spent her time on her mobile and laptop, going over all the design choices for the bakery renovations.

New bakery.

New name.

New start.

The Spiced Phoenix Bakery, Shanti's idea of a clever joke, would reopen by December 1st at the latest. Shanti handled all those details. Akash had learned as a teen never to argue with his baby sister; she'd been a force to be reckoned with from the moment she could speak.

Akash didn't mind. With her design courses at university and part-time work, Shanti had contacts he didn't. Their father always taught his children to work with each other's strengths—stronger together than apart.

"Aki?" Shanti looped her slender arms around his waist. "Are you sure I can't work my magic on your flat as well? Give it a spruce up?"

"No. It's fine. A bit of smoke, but no need to gut the place. We aired it out. Keep your renovating obsession out of it." Akash stood his ground on the issue despite her narrowed gaze. "What's wrong with my flat?"

"It's duller than your wardrobe."

Ouch.

"Harsh." Akash tugged on a strand of her hair. "Ganesh doesn't mind my flat."

"He's a cat." She spoke slowly and patted her brother's head. "He doesn't care about aesthetics. He wants something to scratch, somewhere to use the loo, and a place to sleep."

The arrival of the woman from his insurance company interrupted the pointless conversation. Shanti dragged Nye and Hamish outside with her. Akash walked around with the woman, who approved all the work they had done and what they intended to do for renovations.

Contractors would arrive on the following Monday. His flat had been declared liveable once more. Akash found himself oddly reluctant to leave Hamish's place.

Don't I want my own space again? Yes. Will I miss sleeping in his bed? Definitely. Am I being a total twat? Naturally.

"Well?" Shanti danced in, with Nye and Hamish following sedately behind her. "What did she say? Everything good?"

"Flat's clear. Work starts Monday." Akash avoided the unwavering gaze of the blue-eyed marine looming behind his sister and her boyfriend. "They accepted all of your suggestions."

"Of course they did. I'm brilliant." Shanti smiled brightly at her brother. She glanced over her shoulder at Hamish with a calculating gaze. "Let's celebrate. Nye and I will grab a takeaway for us all. We'll be back in a tick."

"Subtle." Akash rolled his eyes, watching his sister lead Nye out with her hand firmly gripping his. He exchanged an amused smile with Hamish. "She's never found a reason to develop quiet tact. She's too charming to need it. I'll move back into my flat over the weekend."

"Fine." Hamish's smile faltered slightly.

Great.

Now it's gone all rom-com awkward.

Akash floundered for a way to explain his hopes for them.

"We'll see each other, of course."

Oh yes, that's settled it right out.

Why am I suddenly so useless?

Hamish backed Akash against the nearest wall, stalking after him. His teeth caught the edge of Akash's earlobe. "Oh yes, *Aki.* We'll see plenty of each other. You're mine. All mine. No intentions of disappearing now we've finally got started."

"Well." Akash cleared his throat, then ran his tongue across his lips. "Glad we've sorted that out."

"Thrilled." Hamish used his uninjured arm to pin him in place. "We'll celebrate on our own tonight at my flat."

Akash shivered in anticipation, half-hard at the vivid flashes his imagination conjured up. They'd done a few things since he'd moved in with Hamish, and each time they were together it felt hotter than the last. "Can't wait."

Hamish rested his forehead against Akash's with their lips apart and their breath mingling. "Aren't you bakers good at being patient?"

"Never want the dough to be overproved."

"Never."

"Oi. Keep it covered. I'm not interested in being scarred for life." Shanti broke into their staring match. "Hasn't there been enough fire in here?"

CHAPTER TWENTY-ONE

HAMISH

His flat had never seemed silent or massive until Akash returned to his own place. Hamish didn't know what to do with himself initially. It was ridiculous, given the baker hadn't stayed with him for long.

Unrest in South Sudan in and around the capital distracted him sufficiently. Hamish closely watched the trouble developing, telling himself not to worry. Trace, Lily, and Vinnie could handle themselves.

The lead doctor on the mission had insisted on at least two more weeks of vaccinations and surgeries. The group always worked in the direst situations. Hamish admired their courage; his focus remained on deciding if a larger security presence was required at the compound.

Uneasiness gnawed at his belly, enough for Hamish to text Trace to keep an eye out. They only had a few weeks left on the mission, and those were usually the most dangerous. *It always goes wrong in the last hours before heading home.* The former Navy SEAL had enough experience to appreciate his intuition.

Wyatt: Heard from the team in Juba?

Hamish: Just texted Trace. Why?

Wyatt: Some of the rioters decided to attack the compound. I got a call from someone at the DWB office in London.

Hamish: Shit.

Wyatt: On my way to give you a lift. Nye's already at the office. We'll get a better idea of what's going on and if we should head out there—or tell them to come home.

Hamish: Stop texting and driving.

Wyatt: Yes mother.

"Navy wanker." Hamish frowned at his mobile. He had few rules for their employees, one being never to endanger others by being stupid. Texting and driving certainly fell into that category. "Bloody Yank."

Setting his phone aside, Hamish rushed to change out of his T-shirt into a button-up work shirt. He sent a text to his contact at the foreign office to see if they'd heard anything. *Sodding mouse. I should be there right now.* Shirking his duties always bothered him immensely, even if an injury had been the cause of it.

Twenty minutes of exchanging messages with various sources brought his stress levels down a few notches. Lily swore up and down all the "overexcited male tossers" had exaggerated the situation. They'd had a few rocks thrown, a few windows smashed, and one vehicle torched. Not ideal, but not an emergency in her eyes.

Over their years in service together, Hamish had come to trust Lily's instincts over just about everyone else's, including his own. He could almost hear her shouting at Vinnie and Trace not to be jumpy twats. She'd once shouted down a superior officer in Afghanistan—Nye never let him live it down, either.

Deciding to wait for Wyatt downstairs, Hamish locked up his flat and made his way downstairs. He regretted his decision when a fist caught him by surprise as he stepped out of the building. *What the bloody hell?* Rolling quickly out of the way of the legs beside him, he ignored the flash of pain from his shoulder and jaw to get to his feet.

"You." Hamish rubbed his jaw, moving it around gingerly to ensure nothing had been broken. He stared at the obviously drunk Scottie in front of him. "What the *bloody hell* do you think you're doing?"

"Dunno." Scottie stumbled back against the brick wall. "You're a fucking fuckwit."

"Me?" Hamish kept an arm's length between them. He had no intention of taking another punch, but it seemed wrong to beat on an inebriated man, even if he was a total arse. Scottie's apparent attitude change in helping clean up the bakery hadn't lasted very long at all. "Did you decide to stop stalking Akash and do it to me instead?"

"He's mine."

"Akash isn't an object you can own. He's made his

disinterest in you quite obvious." Hamish worked his jaw gently as it started to stiffen up. "Why the hell am I arguing with a drunken twat? Go the fuck home. I'll call you a cab— or walk for all I care."

"Fucking posh fuckwit." Scottie glowered at him, or a spot to his left in any case. "You're no better than I am."

"I'm sober. I'm sure it helps." Hamish watched dispassionately when the drunk lost his footing and fell back against the wall. Scottie ended up sitting on the ground, slouched against the bricks. "I don't have time to deal with you right now. If I call a cab for you, will you go home?"

"Fuck off."

Hamish found himself reminded of an old military mate who'd died overseas. She'd had a terrible childhood and dealt with it by snapping out at anyone who tried to get close to her. He crouched in front of Scottie, who continued to glare blearily at him. "You sort yourself out, you hear me? I won't have you taking your rage at life out on everyone around you. So sort yourself out."

"Or what?"

Hamish allowed a little of what Nye liked to refer to as the devil in him to show. He felt the cold wrath he used on the battlefield fill him. "I'll have to help you. You don't want my help—not in this. I've no patience for it, and I've no emotional attachment to your sorry arse."

"Fuck off."

"Gladly." Hamish glanced behind him when lights flashed on them, to see Wyatt had pulled up. "Go home, stop drinking yourself into the grave, and find a better way to deal with your memories."

After getting into Wyatt's vehicle, Hamish pulled out his mobile to text a friend who ran a cab company in Cardiff. He'd send one of his larger blokes to get Scottie safely home. The drunken club owner was a problem for another day.

He's not my problem.

"Something I should worry about?" Wyatt asked once Hamish tucked his mobile into his pocket.

"Remember Ruth?"

Wyatt tapped his fingers against the steering wheel while they waited at the light. "Redhead? Tall, angry fucking woman, ran head first into a room we hadn't cleared and got shot dead as a result?"

Hamish winced at the callous summary, though he couldn't argue with it. "We joined up at about the same time. Scottie has the same anger that she had, with the same reasons for it."

"And you couldn't help her, so you want to help him?" Wyatt heaved an exaggeratedly loud and long sigh. "Do we have to? Is he worth it?"

"Yes. Probably not." Hamish pulled down the visor to check on his jaw. "In her memory."

They found Nye already at the office. He'd made a pot of coffee and brought a few packets of biscuits. Hamish grabbed a mug and a packet for himself.

"Hamish?"

He lifted his head from his desk, swiping his hand across his eyes to clear them. He yawned widely despite the sore jaw. "What?"

Akash stepped into view. "Shanti called me to say Nye'd

left in the middle of the night. How long have you been at work? Did something happen?"

"Nothing, as it turns out." Hamish grimaced at the disaster his desk had become. He carefully pushed the cold cup of coffee to the side, and shoved biscuit crumbs along with the crumpled packet into the rubbish bin. "What time is it?"

"A quarter after eight." He walked around the desk to stand behind Hamish's chair, looping his arms around him and resting his cheek on top of Hamish's head. "Why don't I take you out for breakfast?"

"Don't let me fall asleep in my eggs." Hamish tilted his head up, and Akash kissed his forehead. "Good morning."

"Morning." Akash caught sight of his jaw and moved around to stand in front of his chair. "Walk into a door?"

"Scottie's fist."

"Scottie's fist." Akash touched his fingers gently to the bruise. "Thought he'd gotten over his shit."

"Apparently not." Hamish waved a hand, not wanting to have his morning ruined by thoughts of the drunken former rugby player. "I've an idea on how to handle it."

"So have I."

Hamish found the stony glare from the baker arousing and slightly terrifying. He'd seen hardened military veterans who couldn't manage such a look. "A conversation for later, I think. You didn't come here to chat about Scottie."

"Breakfast."

Hamish got to his feet, smiling when Akash didn't move and they ended up with their thighs pressed together with the desk behind him. "Why don't we pick something up to take to my place? I could use a bath."

"The doctor—"

Hamish had exercised as much patience as he intended to with regards to waiting. "I intend to have breakfast with you—then have you. Any complaints?"

"Yes, I'd rather not hear about it." Wyatt spoke from the door.

"*Earp.*" Hamish rested his forehead against Akash's shoulder to keep from leaping across the desk at his old friend. "What do you want?"

"Lily called."

Hamish promptly turned around to give Wyatt his full attention. "And?"

"They've booked flights out for next week." Wyatt leant against the doorframe. His eyes twinkled in such a way that Hamish knew he hadn't heard the last of the teasing. "I've a feeling the doctors decided not to risk an incident. They've pushed up the surgeries they had scheduled."

Hamish rested his hand on Akash's lower back, fingers dipping into the waistband of his jeans. "They'll be planning another visit out there in a few months. You've got to admire their courage."

Wyatt gave a shrug. "No fucking in your office, you hear me?"

"Another word from you and I'll tell your husband." Hamish threatened Wyatt with the one thing guaranteed to at least temporarily get good behaviour from the man. "Go home. Tell Nye to take off as well. We can take the day off. There's nothing important planned."

"Yeah, yeah." Wyatt winked at both of them, then took off with a parting shot. "Use condoms, so the cleaning people don't have to clean up your mess."

"Did he just—" Akash broke into uncontrollable laughter. He clung to Hamish to keep from slipping to the floor. "Let's go have breakfast."

Hamish couldn't help himself. Those deep brown eyes sparkled brightly with laughter. He caught Akash roughly by the hair to drag him up the short distance between them, crushing their lips together, only releasing him when his vision started to blur from a lack of oxygen. "Do you know why I shut the office down for the day?"

"You're getting too old for all-nighters?" Akash teased.

Hamish tugged hard on the younger man's hair, causing him to inhale sharply and buck slightly against the thigh thrust between his legs. He leant down to murmur gruffly against his ear, "I intend to take you hard all day—carry you off on wave after wave of pleasure until you can't even remember your name. I'm going to exhaust you with it."

Akash breathed raggedly while practically rutting against Hamish's thigh. "Fuck."

"Yes, that as well." Hamish caught him by the shoulder to ease him back. "Breakfast first."

CHAPTER TWENTY-TWO

AKASH

Breakfast went by in a complete blur. Akash couldn't actually recall eating anything. He had, though; the smudge of jam on his shirt proved it.

As Hamish hadn't and couldn't have driven to work, Akash drove them to breakfast and to Hamish's flat. He didn't remember the trip from the restaurant to the apartment either. It was a bit worrying when he thought about it.

Standing completely naked in Hamish's bedroom, it occurred to Akash that perhaps his brain might've kicked in a little earlier. It had all come into sharp focus once both men stripped down to nothing. He rested his hands on his hips for something to do with them, not wanting to fidget nervously in front of the man sitting on the edge of the bed.

His lips were swollen. They'd obviously exchanged kisses. His cock was hard enough to roll out dough. Hamish had him all mixed up.

"Come here." Hamish crooked a finger at him. "Closer."

Akash stopped just out of arm's reach, and Hamish leant out to catch him by the wrist to drag him the rest of the way. "Watch your shoulder."

"Let me worry about it," Hamish replied confidently. "It's healed up enough."

Scooting back on the bed, Hamish gestured for Akash to straddle his lap. His stomach tightened when his cock wound up against the hardened stomach of the Royal Marine, whose own shaft pressed along Akash's arse. *Gods, this is slow, unending torture. No wonder I tried to block it out.* The cruel man underneath him chuckled when he rocked forward.

Hamish brought his hand up to cup the back of Akash's neck. He applied pressure until Akash had to lower his head. "Sure you're ready?"

"Ready enough to burst. You can stop asking." Akash didn't know if his patience could handle any more questioning. He appreciated the respect, but their foreplay had lasted for months, through a trip overseas and an injured shoulder. "I just want to fuck."

"Fair enough."

Oh, my gods, I said that aloud.

The ground will swallow me whole, and I won't have to look into those smug eyes.

Akash glanced down to find bemused blue eyes staring straight up at him. "Why me?"

Moment of humiliation aside, Akash relished finally having his naked body flush against the man he'd been lusting over for months and months. His eyes stayed on Hamish's, but his fingers strayed all over the upper body laid bare for him. He'd seen him in the bath, of course; it hadn't been like this though.

His cock wasn't all but rammed into me then—makes it a bit different.

Wish it was rammed in me.

His fingers explored a long scar across Hamish's collarbone. An old wound. His eyes asked the obvious question, but Hamish only shook his head. It was clearly not something to ask about now.

He'd learn about the scars. They'd discover each other's scars. He hoped.

The quiet exploration continued for long minutes. Akash rocked gently between Hamish's stomach and the heavy weight of the shaft behind him. Their lips met over and over for increasingly deep kisses.

Hamish dropped his hands to Akash's waist, lifted him up, and tossed him into the bed. He got to his feet. "Have you been a good lad? Not playing around while I was gone."

"You're—" Akash choked on his word when Hamish chose to flick the inside of his thigh. "I do *not* have a pain fetish."

"Your cock jumped a mile." Hamish rubbed the tender skin he'd flicked. "Are you sure?"

With a smirk, Hamish caught Akash by the ankle to drag him around on the mattress until he almost hung off the edge. He stepped between his legs, lifting them up so Akash had to wrap them around him. Their shafts rested on top of each other, and Hamish wrapped both of his hands around them to stroke them together.

Akash gripped the taller man by the legs to hold himself up and watch those capable fingers gliding up and down. "Shouldn't feel so good."

Hamish swirled a finger along both heads. "Yes, it should."

His body had been on edge since their first kiss. The calloused fingers drove him closer and closer. His body tightened, only for him to groan when the hands disappeared, leaving him cruelly yards from the finish line.

"Shift up." Hamish swatted him on the thigh and helped him lower his legs. "I've plans for you, yet."

"Do they involve your cock in me?" Akash stumbled slightly getting to his feet, only to be shoved back onto the mattress. He leant up on his elbows to watch Hamish dig around in one of his nightstands. "What are you doing?"

"One should *always* be properly prepared." Hamish returned to the bed with a condom already on his cock and a bottle of lube in his hand; he lay between Akash's legs, spreading them wide. "Always."

It went agonisingly slowly. Akash worried he might lose his mind if things didn't speed up a little. He felt as if every nerve in his body was on edge waiting for the climax.

Any damn climax.

In the past, slick fingers would likely have been more than sufficient for him. *Not now.* Akash wanted to feel Hamish inside of him. He had done all the waiting he intended to do.

"I'm not a sodding virgin." Akash snapped at him, tired

of playing around. "How much preparation do you think is required?"

Hamish twisted his fingers around even more slowly than he'd been doing. "I enjoy a bit of foreplay, Aki."

"You enjoy fucking torture." Akash dropped his head back against the mattress with a groan. "You're killing me."

"Killing you?" Hamish pressed further in with his fingers. "I haven't even started yet. You'll be beautiful while I take you apart; push you further over the edge than you've ever been."

"Fuck."

"I'll learn every single thing you can't resist, and I'll *never* forget how to make you weak." Hamish eased his fingers out only to push in with his shaft. "Stunning."

Their lips met with every downward thrust. Akash briefly wondered how this would affect Hamish's injured shoulder. The thought flew out of his mind on a fire of pleasure surging through him.

The blessed heat in him disappeared. Akash didn't get a chance to complain about it. He found himself flipped over on his stomach and yanked to the edge of the mattress.

With Akash's knees spread and resting on the edge, Hamish drove into him once again. His fingers caught Akash's, pulling his arms back. It provided leverage to truly pick up the pace.

Hamish eventually released his hands to allow Akash's arms to drop down to the mattress. "Stroke yourself."

With his body on auto-pilot, Akash reached underneath his body to begin to stroke his aching hard-on. He couldn't believe either of them had lasted as long as they had. The thought barely crossed his mind when his orgasm hit hard enough to send him face first on the mattress, woozy and breathless. Hamish collapsed on top of him moments later, having been brought over the edge with him.

Their ragged breathing mingled together for several minutes. Hamish rolled over on the bed after carefully easing out of Akash, who started to get up, but the larger man threw an arm across his chest to keep him prone on the mattress.

Akash slowly returned to himself. He breathed deeply until he no longer sounded as if he'd run a marathon. "I envy your eidetic memory if you're going to have this in all its glory forever."

Hamish shifted on his side to look down at Akash. "The day isn't over—and I've only begun to create all the wonderful moments I intend to remember."

"Really?" Akash didn't know if he had anything left in him.

"Think you need a bath."

Ah, well, I hope I had a lot of protein for breakfast, I've a feeling I'll need all the energy I can muster.

Fuck.

He really is a highly attractive man.

CHAPTER TWENTY-THREE

HAMISH

Waiting for the water to fill the tub, Hamish tossed the used condom into the rubbish bin in the corner of the bathroom. He gingerly rolled his shoulders. A day of sex likely hadn't been on the approved list of physical therapy activities, and his muscles would punish him for it, but he had no regrets.

A sound at the door drew his attention. Hamish turned to find Akash, still naked, holding a glass of water in one hand and a couple pills in the other. *Paracetamol.* His lover apparently already knew him well enough to know he'd refuse any strong pain medication; he'd yet to touch the stuff his doctor had prescribed.

Akash held both out to him with a stubborn glint in his eyes. "The bath might help, but so will this."

Hamish tossed the pills back, swallowing them down before quaffing the water. "Any regrets?"

Akash closed the distance between them. He gently caressed one of the larger scars on Hamish's chest. "Not a one."

The tightness in his chest released almost instantly. Hamish hadn't acknowledged the pressure he'd stupidly put on himself. He knew better than most how expectations had a way of ruining things.

We will not ruin this with any of that bullshit.

"How about you?" Akash turned away to check the temperature of the water in the tub. His question came out in a rush.

Hamish forced his eyes away from the bent-over figure of the baker. *What an arse. What was his question? Shit.* "Pardon?"

"How about you?" Akash glanced over his shoulder with a frown, then smirked. "Will you stop staring at my arse and focus? Do you have any regrets?"

"Have you seen your arse? It's gorgeous." Hamish set the glass on the edge of the sink and stalked up behind the still-bent-over Akash. He breathed out a heartfelt sigh of appreciation when his lower half pressed up against the man. "I can guarantee you this with absolute certainty—I'll never, ever regret having you in my bed and in my life."

"Thought you wanted a bath?" He asked after clearing his throat. The words came out thickly with a slight tremble. "Stop smirking against my back."

Hamish grinned even wider as he bent over to lick a swath

between Akash's shoulders. He bucked his hips up to force his hard shaft between the cheeks of his arse, rocking to glide between them. "Water's a bit too warm to hop in right now. Maybe we should let it cool off for a moment."

Taking Akash by the hand, Hamish guided their hands across the baker's side, down his stomach to grasp his shaft. They stroked him together. Their movements worked in time with the rolling of his hips; it took surprisingly little to bring both of them off.

Akash grimaced slightly when they pulled apart. "I'm definitely in need of a bath now."

Hamish grabbed a flannel, moistened it in the tub, and proceeded to wipe off Akash's back. He teased him briefly, earning a half-hearted glare. "Into the water with you."

When Hamish had bought his flat, he'd changed a few things; one had been to put in a truly massive tub. His tall frame required the extra room. He appreciated the decision even more with Akash stretched out on top of him, head on his shoulder and body easily fitting between his legs.

Akash lifted his head up to lightly brush their lips together, only to drop down once again to nuzzle against Hamish's neck. "Don't let me drown."

"I'll keep an eye out." He wrapped his arms possessively around Akash; his fingers lazily roamed across the lithe-muscled, golden flesh of his back. His body showed the work the baker put into his martial arts training. "Are you falling asleep on me?"

"No." Akash yawned so widely, Hamish winced. "Is Nye serious about my sister?"

Hamish winced again at the question. "No comment."

"*Hamish.*"

"Nye before his injuries? I would've warned him off your sister for her sake. He did a lot of soul-searching afterwards. It forced him to rethink a lot of things. He'll do good by her." Hamish had seen his friend bring himself through the worst life could throw at one. He had no doubts Shanti was in good hands—and more than that, could handle herself. "She'd kick your arse for getting involved."

"True."

When the water began to cool, Akash pushed himself up and clambered out of the tub. Hamish climbed out as well. He retrieved two towels, handing one over and using the second to dry off.

"Tea?" Hamish tossed both damp towels into the laundry basket. "Are you hungry at all?"

"Coffee. All the coffee. So much coffee." Akash tumbled by him out of the bathroom and down the hall. "Coffee."

"Yes, I believe we covered your need for it." Hamish got the kettle on and dropped onto one of the stools around the small island. "Might could use a mug myself."

Sitting at the table, Hamish crossed his arms and rested his chin on them. He'd overdone it. *God, that arse. How could I not?* Exhaustion seeped into him like a vapour and struggled to keep his eyes open.

Akash sat beside him and stretched a hand out to run fingers through Hamish's slightly damp hair. "Is it time for a late lunch or an early supper?"

Hamish couldn't lift his head, leaning toward the fingers

threading through his hair. "No clue."

"How about we have a nap and then a later supper?" Akash chuckled.

"Nap. Good," Hamish muttered drowsily. He blinked in surprise when the kettle whistled. "Coffee? You wanted coffee."

"Later. Up you get." Akash turned off the hob, set the kettle to one side, and guided him through his flat toward the bedroom, where he fell forward onto the mattress. "Right. Going to roll over so I can join you?"

Hamish sat up to grab him by the wrist, and dragged Akash onto the bed. He tucked the man into his arms, rolled on his side to be more comfortable, and immediately started to drift off. "There. Room. Sleep."

CHAPTER TWENTY-FOUR

AKASH

For having moved back into his flat, Akash spent a remarkable amount of time at Hamish's place. Over a couple of weeks, they went out on several dates, almost always winding up in his bed. He couldn't find a reason to complain.

Who would?

The renovations on his bakery had been finished a week early. It would reopen in a few days, on Friday morning. Akash initially planned to simply go on with business as usual, but Shanti convinced him to at least post a few flyers about the neighbourhood.

He didn't see the point. All of his customers followed him online, where he'd kept them all up to date on the progress of the renovations. He planned to create a few special pastries for the occasion.

Might as well.

Slouched down in a chair in the rebuilt kitchen, Akash jotted notes down in his chef's journal, a habit he'd picked up from one of his baking mentors. He kept a careful diary of every recipe created, or at the very least tweaked by him; he didn't have Hamish's brilliant ability to never forget. Luck had been on his side the night of the fire, and his book had been in his vehicle.

Unlike his Royal Marine, Akash tended to forget all the important things, but remembered every single humiliating moment of his life. Grabbing his now cold cup of tea, he moved over to the sink to dump it out. He decided to make his way down the street to the café on the corner for a cup of coffee and a sandwich. Maybe it would inspire him to come up with an extra-special creation for his bakery.

After double-checking the back door, Akash headed out the front of the bakery. He locked up, waving at the owner of the shop beside his. She smiled and wished him luck on the opening, promising to come over if only to get her usual scone.

"Oi. Akash. Wait up."

Akash groaned at Scottie's familiar voice, and continued on toward the café, hoping the man would take his lack of interest as a sign to go away. "Not likely."

"Talking to yourself?" Scottie caught up with him. "Will you slow the fuck down? I want to talk to you."

"Not interested."

Scottie shot in front of him to halt his forward momentum.

"Look—"

"No." Akash squared off against Scottie for what seemed like the millionth time. "Will you bugger off? I'm *not* interested."

"Sit your ass down." A grey-haired and bearded man who stood about two inches taller than Scottie moved between them. "You hear me? I said to sit your punk ass down."

Akash frowned when the American stranger grabbed Scottie by the shoulder and shoved him onto the kerb. "I was handling it."

"Is this an exclusive party of three?" Hamish rounded the corner and joined them. He glared at Scottie, who surged up only for the grey-bearded stranger to knock him back down. "Ahh. Gray. I see you've made yourself useful."

"I'll just continue being useful." He grabbed Scottie by the back of the shirt, yanked him up to his feet, and dragged him away.

"What the hell?" Akash watched the retreating figures while trying to process what had happened. "Or, more, who the hell was that?"

"Meet our newest employee—Gray Baird. He'll be quick to tell you it's not pronounced 'Beard' as well. Retired marine and police chief from the States, if the accent didn't give it away. An old friend of Wyatt's. He apparently got bored in the sunshine and decided to join us." Hamish sounded rather unenthused about the arrival of the man. "He doesn't have a lot of patience for what he considers to be stupidity."

"And Scottie?"

"King of stupidity." Hamish shrugged.

Akash decided not to worry about Scottie and focus on more important things. "Shouldn't you both be at work?"

"Showing him around the city and helping him find a flat." Hamish draped his arm across Akash's shoulders. "Want to have lunch with me? Not sure how long Scottie's spanking is going to be."

"He's not actually—" Akash didn't know if he really wanted to know. "I'm having coffee and a bite to eat at the café we tried last week."

"Figure of speech." Hamish led him toward the café. "I hope."

Two coffees and grilled cheese sandwiches later, Akash wandered back toward his bakery with Hamish in tow. They found Gray waiting patiently by the front door. Scottie was nowhere in sight.

"Akash Robinson." He held his hand out toward the American.

"Gray."

Akash blinked at the nod he received in acknowledgement, and let his hand fall to his side. "Right."

Hamish turned his head to wink at Akash. "I've got a few more places to show him. Can I take you out for supper later?"

"Sure."

With a quick, bruising kiss, Hamish strolled away, his new American friend following behind him. Akash rolled his eyes at the two men. He returned to brainstorming recipes, and tried not to think about all the other nonsense going on around him.

Aside from renovating, Akash had lost both of his assistants. The twins found working with Aled in the garden far more peaceful than having to deal with daily customers. They'd stood in his flat fidgeting nervously for ten minutes before Alice blurted out that they loved him but wanted to change jobs.

He'd miss seeing them every day. They promised to come by often. He told them he was proud of them for being brave enough to change their routine up with a new job.

And he was.

The shop would be far quieter without the two of them. Alice tended to hum nonstop, while Alex randomly repeated *Doctor Who* quotes. He felt like a big brother letting his younger siblings go for the first time.

Stop being daft.

Grabbing his mobile, Akash messaged a reminder to himself to follow up with the university to see if they had any students to recommend to him. They'd promised him a few candidates. He hoped one or two would be willing to start immediately.

His mum had made him promise never to attempt to run the bakery alone for more than a day or two. He'd once wound up exhausting himself to the point of needing to go to the hospital. It only made him want to work on his endurance.

Mum worries too much.

The good news was, the twins had emailed him earlier. They'd come in to help him prepare everything the morning of the opening. Akash knew not to ask them to stay for the crowds; people loved to gossip, and going to the reopening of a shop after an arson attack provided plenty of opportunity for them.

As long as the gossips bought scones and pasties, Akash couldn't be bothered to worry over the rumours spread about him. He hadn't heard anything from detectives. No arrests had been made.

They knew it was arson, and that Akash hadn't done it.

Freddie: Have any plans for the evening?

Akash: Of a sort. Why?

Freddie: Want to go to the Sin Bin with us?

Akash: Us?

Freddie: Everyone involved with the club and their significant others, except for Caddock because Francis can't handle the free-flowing alcohol.

Freddie: Bring your marine. Aled's coming as well with Wyatt.

Akash: Scottie might not be so pleased by all of this.

Freddie: Taine said not to worry about it.

Odds of this all ending badly? Ten to one. Shit.

His imaginary plans for the evening evaporated immediately. No supper, no evening alone in Hamish's flat. They'd have a quick bite before going to the club. He hoped everyone behaved themselves.

Akash: Slight change of plans. Want to go to the Sin Bin with me tonight?

Hamish: Only to spend time with you. Can I bring backup?

Akash: Backup?

Hamish: Gray found Scottie amusing.

Akash: I don't want to know.

Hamish: Pick you up at six for supper before we head to the club? Wyatt can bring the others with him.

CHAPTER TWENTY-FIVE

HAMISH

With his physical therapy and stubbornness, Hamish managed to recover much of the use of his shoulder in the first few weeks. He wouldn't be at full whack for another four or five weeks, but at least he could drive himself places. It had rankled not being able to control his own movements.

The doctor in Juba had told him quite specifically not to do anything strenuous. *Does having sex multiple times a day count? Probably.* His Cardiff doctor quite adamantly informed him not to even think about working out beyond the physical therapy. He couldn't be bothered to worry.

Leaving any lifting of weights, aside from Akash, Hamish kept his workout focused mostly on his lower body. He jogged instead of his usual intense daily run. His mind and body required consistency to stay sharp.

Soft targets take the first hits.

I'm no good to anyone if I'm not at my best.

He definitely had to be at his best for a night at the Sin Bin.

On a scale of one to ten, Hamish found his interest in dancing the night away to be off the charts in the negative. The only draw was Akash. Any evening spent with his baker was well worth potential aggravation from the persistent pest named Scottie.

With all their employees in Cardiff for a few days, Hamish told Wyatt to invite all of them for a well-earned night out at the club. They'd also serve as a buffer zone between him and Scottie. His previous visit had ended in a fight, and hopefully this time would be less volatile.

In the end, Hamish could only control himself. Scottie's behaviour didn't exactly come under his purview. Maybe the man had finally learned his lesson, with Gray practically schooling him like a child.

Doubtful.

After a quick shower following his run, Hamish dressed to impress in a striking midnight blue suit with a crisp white button-up, no tie. Akash's jaw-dropping told him the choice had been a wise one. The desperate way his lover dragged him into a kiss spoke volumes as well.

Wanting the evening to begin on a good note, Hamish had made reservations at Chapel 1877. Akash had been drooling over the restaurant for days after Shanti told him about her visit with Nye. They greatly enjoyed their supper of lamb and sea bass, sharing bites between them.

Arms wound around each other, they made their way from Chapel 1877 across to where he'd parked. Hamish couldn't resist Akash in his tight trousers. He held him against the side of the vehicle, a captive more than ready for a kiss if the gleam in his eyes meant anything.

Akash tasted of wine and the decadent chocolate ice cream they'd shared. He laughed a bit breathlessly when Hamish released him. "Thought we'd had our pudding already. Are you developing a sweet tooth?"

"In the Mercedes, before we get ourselves in trouble." Hamish made sure to drag his knee across Akash's front, earning himself a kick in the arse for his troubles. "Careful."

"I'm the very picture of cautious." Akash winked at him before climbing into the vehicle. He dropped a hand on Hamish's thigh once he'd gotten settled behind the wheel. "Thank you."

"For?"

Akash shook his head and turned his eyes toward the road. "Just thanks."

They drove the short distance from the restaurant to the club. Freddie had texted them to say Taine suggested they park in the employee lot to save time and aggravation. Given the line outside the front door, Hamish appreciated the thought.

"Wait." Akash caught his arm when he reached for the seat belt. "When I said thank you earlier?"

Hamish released his seat belt and twisted in the seat to face Akash. "Yes?"

"You read my blog."

He shifted his shoulder slightly to ease the tension in them before trying to decipher what Akash was talking about. "Ah. The restaurant."

After Shanti's visit to the restaurant, Akash had used her photos of the food to talk about his eating out wish list on his bakery blog. Hamish hadn't wanted to admit how he checked every day to see if it updated. *Intel gathering.* He had no qualms about using every tool at his disposal to learn about the man.

Akash brushed a few stray hairs from his trousers, likely from Ganesh. He opened his mouth and closed it, swiping once again at his clothes as if to gather his thoughts. "This might be something special—you and me."

"Might be?"

"Too early to be certain." Akash finally lifted his eyes to meet Hamish's. "Break my heart, and I'll demonstrate how well I learned both aikido and Krav Maga."

Hamish didn't do Akash the disservice of laughing at his threat. He had no doubts they'd be evenly matched if they ever chose to spar. *Might be fun naked with a bit of oil.* "Don't give me your heart—I haven't earned it yet."

Akash struggled with his seat belt before getting it to release. He glared at Hamish when he chuckled. "You've ruined the moment."

"Have I?" Hamish leant across the console, and his fingers found familiar purchase in the hair on the back of Akash's head. He loved using the silky, dark strands to control the man. "I'm confident we can find it again."

Whenever Hamish tugged sharply on Akash's hair, his eyes tended to darken, and his breathing became ragged. His mouth opened, waiting for the kiss. Hamish held him still to taunt him with light flicks of his tongue across the baker's bottom lip.

"*Please.*"

Closing the short distance, Hamish claimed the other man's mouth. He thrust his tongue into Akash's mouth, who slid his hands along Hamish's chest to rest on either side of his neck. Their kisses moved swiftly from merely earnest to demanding and sloppy.

After ten minutes of deep, torrid kisses, they collapsed into their seats with bruised lips, wrinkled shirts, and mussed up hair. Hamish couldn't deny a thrill at knowing it would be obvious what they'd been doing. *Maybe not obvious enough.* He latched on to Akash's neck with his lips and teeth, biting down and sucking hard enough to leave no doubts in anyone's mind.

Akash whacked him in the back of the head and pushed him away when he laved at the mark. "I believe your point will be made; no need to belabour it."

They made their way through the rows of parked cars, down past the line of people trying to get in, to find the doormen already had their names. Hamish caught Akash by the hand. They ducked inside the darkened foyer.

"Hang on. Let me find out where they're all at." Akash led him toward a corner out of the way of the door and fished out his mobile. "Freddie said they've retreated to the second-floor bar."

The Sin Bin had been designed as a three-tiered club. On the first floor was a bar along with space for live music;

tonight it had some new indie sensation that made Hamish's ears bleed. The second had a bar, as well, but usually stuck to more mellow jazz and blues. The third level held the dance floor that he avoided like the plague.

I was not born to dance.

Akash stowed his phone in his pocket and threaded their fingers together again. He led them to the stairs through the double doors into the 1920s-themed bar. "Over there."

Following the nod, Hamish spotted the large circular booth filled with several of their friends. They wound through small groups of people until they reached the table. Hamish ordered a glass of wine for Akash and a tumbler of scotch for himself, and slid into a seat beside him.

"Might want to button up your shirt, Hamster." Wyatt kicked him under the table. "Comb your hair? You'd fail an inspection."

Hamish draped his arm across the back of the booth. "Would I? Not sure you'd pass muster, given your hand is practically down your husband's pants."

"*Hamish.*" Aled's attempt to scold was drowned out by the raucous laughter from almost everyone else at the table. Hamish sent the botanist an apologetic smile, which he waved off with a roll of his eyes.

Wyatt shrugged. "Well, he's not wrong."

Aled pinched the bridge of his nose. "Why did I marry you?"

"The hand on your dick." Trace leapt over the back of the booth before Wyatt could grab him. "Going to the dance floor."

"We'll make sure he doesn't get in trouble." Graham dragged BC with him. "We'll keep Scottie away from the bar."

And away from us.

All the rugby players turned club owners wanted the Sin Bin to be a success. The lines outside spoke well for their chances, but having a complete arsehole for a manager wouldn't keep the crowds for long. He wondered if they intended to keep a tighter leash on Scottie to prevent any potential problems.

Or give him a complete personality change.

Wyatt kicked him in the shin again to get his attention. "We've got two new contracts that came in after you left."

"Oh?"

"A three-month protection detail on a yacht—Lily and Trace would be a good balance for it." Wyatt waited for his nod of agreement, which he gave readily. The two dealt well with each other. "The other is five months in northern Syria at a medical facility. An anonymous donor paid for our services. We're trading out with another security group who has been there for eight months."

"How big of a team?" Hamish didn't necessarily want to disappear for five months, but needs must. "When does it start?"

"Four or five. So all hands on deck for it. We'd leave in three weeks, which is plenty of time for your fucking shoulder to be healed up enough. Check with your doctor first, though." Wyatt raised his glass in a mock salute. "I've got those training courses you lined up for me, so I can't go. You, Scorch, Vinnie, and Voodoo should manage it fine. Nye and Gray can stay with me to keep the world from collapsing around us."

"Nye won't like it." Hamish knew exactly how his old friend would take being sidelined. "He'll think we don't trust him."

"Client was incredibly specific. Good fucking luck with them." Wyatt downed the rest of his drink before glancing at his husband. "We should dance."

Eventually, everyone filtered to the third floor of the club. Hamish stayed with Akash, nursing their drinks and chatting about what his being gone for five months would mean for them. They'd managed fine with emails and Skype before, so he didn't a see a reason for this to be any different.

They'd been getting to know each other at the time. Hamish knew Akash had concerns. They'd grown so much closer; being apart would be infinitely harder.

Friends came and went throughout their first hour at the club. They'd drink, then return to dancing or the live concert. Hamish watched Akash with growing amusement; he had a feeling they'd be joining those on the third floor soon.

"Dance with me?" Akash pulled Hamish out of the booth. "We might as well brave the masses with everyone else."

"Do you dance?" Hamish stumbled against a table, but righted himself as they moved out of the bar. "What's life without a little adventure?"

"Says the man who dislocated his shoulder tripping over a dormouse," Akash retorted playfully.

"Fair point." Hamish pushed him into the corner of the stairwell, needing a kiss, however brief, to fortify himself. "You've no complaints about how I move everywhere else. Why should dancing be any different?"

"We're being whistled at." Akash ducked under his arms and caught him by the hand to lead him by the idiots catcalling them. "Let's find the others before we cause a scene."

"Wouldn't be the first time." Hamish didn't mind causing a scene at all. "I doubt they'd kick us out."

"Scottie would."

Hamish would have a few choice words for the club manager if he dared to bother them. "We'll handle him if he decides to be an arse."

CHAPTER TWENTY-SIX

For all his many faults, Scottie ran a tight ship at the Sin Bin. The music didn't deafen, the lights didn't blind, and the staff kept up with empty glasses and spilt drinks; the heavily muscled bouncers closely monitored who made it inside, likely not wanting to risk any illicit activities leading to them being shut down. It had definitely become a favourite club to visit for many.

As most of their former rugby playing friends stood head and shoulders above the rest of the world, Akash easily spotted them close to the DJ booth set up against the far left wall of the room. He started toward them, only for Hamish to pull him back to his side. They instead lost themselves in the crowd of bodies moving to the music; his partner eased him into his arms, swaying to the sensual rhythm of the music.

To his immense surprise, Hamish kept up with him through song after song. Akash expected him to tire after the first song, or at least to balk at some of the music. Fast or slow, the blond seemed determined to enjoy the evening to the fullest.

Of the three Robinson siblings, Shanti was definitely the one to enjoy spending time at a club. *Not me, and Padma would rather shave her entire head than come out to a place like this.* Akash often went with his little sister to keep her out of trouble. She usually ended up being the one to rescue him from her salivating friends, who refused to grasp his lack of interest in them.

A clenching of Hamish's jaw drew his attention. Akash noticed belatedly how tight the man held himself. His shoulder had clearly begun to hurt again. Taking him by the hand, he led the slightly taller man through the crowd over to the small bar on the opposite side of the room.

Akash ordered a pint and bottled water for both of them. Alcohol didn't hydrate; his father always stressed the importance of drinking something non-alcoholic on a night out. "Are you all danced out yet?"

"Not really." Hamish grabbed one of the square napkins to wipe the sweat from his brow. "Did you want to leave already?"

He didn't want to go, not yet. Leaving would mean facing the fact of Hamish preparing for another sojourn away, and in a far more dangerous place. It made him wonder if this was the stress and worry his mother had suffered through while his father had been active in the military.

His father hadn't served in any highly volatile places. Hamish would be in the middle of one of the most explosive regions of the world at the moment. Akash knew the next five months would involve a massive amount of meditation for him.

A concern for another day.

And speaking of concerns.

"I'm going to find the loo." Akash squeezed by Hamish, rubbing his body against his lover's. "You up for more dancing when I get back?"

"I'm certainly up for something," Hamish grumbled.

The line for the toilets seemed as long as the one to get inside the club. Akash waited patiently for his turn, cursing whoever decided to not have urinals but only stalls. The delay, unfortunately, caused him to run straight into Scottie on his way back to Hamish.

"Akash." Scottie blocked the doors when he tried to step around him. "Can I buy you a drink?"

"No." Akash pondered the pros and cons of kicking the owner of the club in the balls. "Are you completely daft? Is 'no' a concept you are unfamiliar with? This isn't a fucking Jane Austen novel where your arseholishness will be redeemed in the end."

"Who the fuck are you talking about?" Scottie brought his arms up to keep the door closed. "What's the harm in one drink? It's just a beer. I'm not asking to fuck you in the stairwell."

"Move."

"One drink," Scottie hissed harshly. His folded his arms

across his chest, leaning forward towards Akash. "You can have whatever you fucking want."

"Not if my life depended on it." Akash planted his feet, twisting his body slightly while forcing his shoulders and arms to relax. He clenched his fists at his sides. "You've one second to get out of my way."

"Or what?"

Akash counted to ten in three languages to hold his temper at bay. He remembered his father always telling him never to strike in anger. "Or I'll kick you in the bollocks hard enough you'll still be tasting them for breakfast on Monday."

"Do you ever learn, punk?"

Akash risked a glance to his right to find the imposing figure of Gray. The man's stony glare focused entirely on Scottie. "He doesn't. Do you mind?"

His question had been meant for Scottie. Gray apparently decided it was directed at him. He once again grabbed the temperamental former rugby player and dragged him away, struggling and cursing the whole way.

Well, that's a disaster in the making. Hope I'm around to see the fireworks.

In his absence, Hamish had been joined by their friends, who were all flushed from exertion and wanting refreshments. Akash squashed himself between his lover and the table. He received a lick on the back of his neck for his effort.

Idiot.

Hamish looped an arm around him and dropped his head on Akash's shoulder. "Thought you got lost in the crowd or fell into the loo."

"Long lines and a clueless wanker." Akash ordered another beer for himself since someone had swanned off with the one he'd left. "Are we done in for the night, then?"

"I'm officially too old for this shit." Wyatt dropped his head on the table, and his husband reached over to rest a hand against his neck. "Anyone hungry? I could eat a fucking horse. Is that sandwich place open across the street? We need coffee before any of us are getting behind the wheel."

"It's open." BC pulled away from Graham long enough to answer. "Oi. Tens."

The half-Maori, half-Scot wandered over with Freddie in tow. It didn't take long for Remi and Sarah to join them. Akash had only met the French man and his Cornish wife once before; they tended to be the quietest of the group.

Slowly everyone joined them. They chatted over the last of their drinks until BC convinced them all to walk across the street. The club had started to fill up with a slightly younger crowd. Akash got the sense most of them didn't have the patience to deal with the loud and chaotic dancers.

To no one's surprise, Remi and Sarah begged off. They'd be driving to Boscastle in the morning to check on her brother, Ivan; they grabbed one of the cabs lined up outside of the Sin Bin. Akash preferred not to shove his nose into their personal business, but he'd heard Graham mention the troubles in passing.

"Late snack or home to bed?" Hamish asked when they'd stepped out into the cold night air. "They won't miss us."

They would.

They'd tease endlessly about it.

Akash didn't care; somehow seeing all the lights already set up in preparation for December had sobered him up. "You'll miss New Year's."

"Maybe. Probably. Might be gone before Christmas." Hamish wrapped an arm around his shoulders and walked in silence. He probably didn't want to think about his upcoming travels yet. "My flat or yours?"

Akash gestured toward the group heading across the street to the coffee shop. "Let's grab a coffee first, yeah? Make sure we're safely sober."

And I'll put my mind to thinking of a way to give you a proper send-off, so you'll have something to remind you of why you've got to come home safely.

CHAPTER TWENTY-SEVEN

HAMISH

Stretched out on his bed with Akash on his side beside him, Hamish closed his eyes in an attempt to doze off. It didn't work. His mind refused to let go of several conversations from the last few hours.

Over coffee and sandwiches, Wyatt had brought up the fact that several of their group would miss the holidays. They'd come to the conclusion that any of the company who'd be gone in December should have the next week off to spend time with their family. *If they want it, who am I going to see?*

Akash.

He's about the only one.

Christmas didn't matter much to Hamish, not with his immediate family gone. No one cared if he followed all their time-honoured traditions. He hadn't celebrated much in the past few years, though Lily or Nye often invited him over to theirs, so he wasn't alone.

Until Akash mentioned it, being gone by the end of December hadn't mattered much one way or the other. Hamish was slapped in the face by the realisation that for the first time in a while he had someone to leave behind. Not a family member, not a friend, but a lover who would worry about him and miss him.

I'll have to update my letter.

When his parents were alive, his commanding officer kept a letter written by him to be sent to his family in the case of his death. His goodbyes. Most of the men and women who served did the same thing. They never wanted to leave any words unsaid if the worst happened. *Always say your I love yous and your goodbyes.*

He hadn't penned one in a while. Friends wouldn't appreciate it the same way. He thought now he'd found someone who might actually need words of comfort if his return trip was in a wooden box in the cargo hold of a plane.

God forbid.

Finding sleep impossible, Hamish snuck out of bed. He left Akash snoring lightly and grabbed his laptop off the dresser. The thought of not having a letter ate away at him, and rest wouldn't come until he'd made an attempt at it.

Hamish sat for an hour staring at a blank document. He eventually found at least the right place to start. A poem he'd memorised in school came to him, and it seemed to somehow speak to what he wanted to say.

Dear Akash,

Not sure why Tennyson's words from "The Charge of the Light Brigade" came to me when I started to write this. "Theirs not to reason why, theirs but to do and die." I've written many versions of this letter over the years. It's never easy to know what are the right words to help the grieving. It's morbid, but the weight we've chosen to carry, so I'll do my best.

If this letter makes it into your hands, I'm already gone—and I'm sorry.

I told you not to give me your heart yet—I hadn't earned it. Trouble is I'd already laid mine in your hands. You treated it with kindness. Thank you.

You've a strength in you, Aki. It's what drew me to you. It's trite and clichéd, but our short time together has felt like a brilliant and beautiful lifetime. If I've a regret, it's that I won't be able to see where we would've gone.

"Hamish?" Akash called out to him from the shadows of the bedroom doorway, his naked form highlighted by the single light in the living room. "Can't sleep?"

Hamish hit Save and quickly shut down his laptop; the rest of his letter could wait for another day. "Too much on my mind. Did I wake you?"

"You've had too much coffee." Akash started to walk by

him toward the kitchen. "My mum swears by warm milk. Maybe with a splash of brandy?"

Hamish caught him by the waist and dragged him over. He pressed their bodies tightly together. "I've a far better idea than hot milk. A bit of warmth will likely be involved."

"Aren't we supposed to be resting? This doesn't feel like resting." Akash followed him readily over to the sofa. "Is the bed too good for you?"

"That's enough out of you. Hold on a minute." Hamish left to retrieve a condom and lube from the bedroom, and returned to find Akash stretched out on his back on the sofa with his arms crossed behind his head. "Gotten all comfy, have we?"

Climbing onto the couch to straddle Akash's legs, Hamish bent forward to make a meal of licking and sucking his way across the bronze-toned upper body laid bare for him. He teased one hard nipple then the other with his fingers, and drew lines with his tongue between them and down Akash's stomach, which tightened when he nipped at his side.

As they'd played around before bed, foreplay was more of a luxury and less of a necessity. Hamish enjoyed the slow build-up. He loved how Akash grew increasingly frustrated with him.

Eventually, though, Hamish took the condom to ready himself and moved up to cover Akash with his body. His arms found purchase on either side of him, keeping him from tumbling off the sofa. Their lips met in a languid exploration.

Akash brought his legs up, and his heels dug into the back of Hamish's legs. He caressed Hamish's thighs. "I'm putting this on the list of activities not likely to help me sleep."

Silencing him with his lips, Hamish ground their shafts together. He finally reached between them to take his cock and guide it into Akash, whose heels dug harder into his thighs, trying to push him in further—faster. He played absently with the baker's black hair; their lips stayed connected in lazy, carnal grazes.

Their noses bumped together. Hamish sunk himself all the way into Akash. He leant up to watch the expressions flitting across the baker's face when he started to thrust harder.

The raw, exquisite pleasure on his face would feed Hamish's dreams during the lonely months without him. His throat clogged up as thoughts of the unfinished letter on his laptop went through his mind. He dropped his head against Akash's forehead and continued to drive into him.

It wasn't enough.

Getting up and carefully easing himself out, Hamish sat up and helped Akash into his lap. They wound their arms around each other as his lover sank down on his shaft. His hands roamed across Akash's back while he rode with a desperate abandon.

Hamish slipped an arm between their bodies to wrap his hand around Akash's erection. He stroked in time with the rise and fall of his body. "Are you ready?"

A sudden primal ache to control the moment grabbed Hamish and refused to let go. He shifted his hold on Akash, forcing him to lift up higher and drop down harder. The fingers around his shaft stroked faster, squeezing him almost too tightly.

"C'mon then, Aki." Hamish relished the shudder from

the other man. Akash trembled in his arms, sunk down on his shaft, both lost in a burst of heated pleasure. "You're so sodding brilliant, and I'm going to fucking miss you."

I am spent in more ways than one.

Bright sunlight shining on his face woke Hamish up out of a deep sleep. He struggled to sit up, only to find Akash stretched out on top of him, the two of them squashed together on the couch. His shoulder ached almost unbearably, and he couldn't help a grimace at the dried, flaky mess on his stomach.

Akash rolled off his body and dropped to the floor before Hamish could stop him. "Shit. I've no recollection of falling asleep."

"We did."

"I'm aware." Akash got to his feet, stretching slowly in an obvious attempt to wake up. "Did we bother to clean up at all?"

Hamish covered his face with his hands to attempt to muffle his laughter. "Not even with a tissue."

"Why are you— Oh my bloody— Did someone forget to discard their condom?" Akash peeled the rubber from his inner thigh where it had obviously slid. "Stop laughing, you wanker."

They both dissolved into helpless laughter. Akash finally regained control of himself and tossed the condom into the rubbish bin in the corner of the room. Hamish watched him wander across his flat, appreciating the way the sun shone on his naked form.

Getting to his feet, Hamish strode by him toward the bedroom. He smirked when Akash chased after him. Nothing loosened up his muscles like a hot shower; sex would simply be the cherry on his sundae.

Their soapy hands meandered across every inch of skin. They traded positions under the showerhead to rinse each other off. Hamish committed it all to his memory so he could remember Akash in vivid detail.

And he would.

Dropping to his knees in the tub, Hamish shifted them both out of the direct spray of the water. He'd done slow and steady. This morning he was ravenous, and only Akash could sate his hunger.

Taking Akash into his mouth, Hamish coaxed him easily to a full erection. He bobbed up and down, licking and sucking. His fingers gripped Akash's balls to lightly play with them.

His other arm stretched underneath to allow him to pump two of his fingers into Akash. The multiple stimuli had Akash gripping him by the shoulders to keep on his feet. His groans filled the bathroom, echoing around the tiled walls.

Drawing his lover closer to the edge, Hamish pulled his mouth off. He moved his hand up quickly to stroke him to completion. Akash's knees went seconds later, and Hamish brought his arm around him to lift him.

Let's not add a concussion to the list of problems we've suffered this year.

Finishing up in the shower, Hamish wrapped a towel around his waist and made his way into the kitchen. Akash wanted to check in at the bakery and on Ganesh. A glance at the clock by the refrigerator told him they had just enough time for breakfast.

Akash joined him several minutes later, fully dressed. He buttered the toast and got the coffee on the table while Hamish served up two simple omelettes. "Do you have time to hang out at the bakery with me?"

Hamish grabbed two bottles of water for them. "I've all the time in the world over the weekend. I told Wyatt last night that I'd be in the office on Monday."

Akash grinned around a mouthful of food. "I should blog about my towel-clad chef."

"No, no you shouldn't." Hamish snatched the mobile out of Akash's hand and set it out of reach. "Eat your eggs."

They ate quietly. Hamish wanted to drown himself in the coffee. He'd require at least two more mugs to get through the day.

"Hamish?"

"Hmm?" He set his coffee down to focus fully on Akash. "Yes?"

Akash absently tore pieces from his toast. "We're a couple, right? It doesn't feel like *dating*, or a quick fuck to get it out of our system."

"It's going to take a lot more 'quick fucks' to get you out of my system." Hamish caught the piece of toast thrown at him in his mouth. "Finish your breakfast. I'll keep you company in the bakery for a bit."

"That *is* a yes, right?"

Yes.

"Eat your breakfast, Aki." Hamish smiled mildly in response to the pointed glare sent his way. "Yes. Daft idiot."

CHAPTER TWENTY-EIGHT

AKASH

As the weather turned colder, the newly reopened bakery glittered brightly with an overabundance of holiday cheer. Shanti insisted on decking the halls, so to speak. She'd brought Nye over on the previous Friday evening, and they'd covered his shop in lights, Santa, and all things Christmas.

It made her happy. Akash decided not to waste his energy arguing with her. He hadn't won a debate with his baby sister from the time she learned how to talk.

The second week of December brought brilliant news in the form of several new employees. They'd come over from the bakery course at one of the local universities. One covered an early morning shift to help Akash open, and the others closed the day with him.

Each month, the university would send over three new victims for a bit of on-the-job experience. Akash intended to find a suitable candidate from within the multitude of student bakers to bring on full-time—an apprentice of sorts to train up to allow him more free time. He planned to keep his eyes open for the possibility, at least.

With a steady flow of helpers, Akash hoped to create a better schedule for himself to avoid burning out. Padma had always driven herself to the brink of exhaustion for her career. He wanted to leave space in his life to enjoy the fruits of his labour.

How can I have time to build a life with Hamish if I'm buried in flour twenty-four hours a day?

Over the three weeks since their evening at the club, the two men had discovered a comfortable routine. They ran together at a park at five in the morning, had breakfast, spent the day apart at work, and shared a late supper afterwards. They usually alternated whose flat they slept at so Ganesh wasn't abandoned.

The two had spent a portion of each day together. Time was short. Hamish had a flight out at the end of the week, and making the most of what was left seemed important. Every evening became a date night, even if at times they were too tired to do more than collapse on the couch and watch the telly together.

And then there was the sex. They'd christened every surface in both of their flats. Hamish's office served as a thrilling addition to their adventures; so had his Mercedes, though it had been slightly uncomfortable.

As the date of Hamish's flight grew closer, Akash grew increasingly more worried. He obsessively watched the news. The situation appeared direr than it had only a month ago.

He'll be fine. He'll be fine. He'll definitely be completely and totally fine.

I hope.

"Mr Robinson?"

"Akash. Call me Akash. I'm not old enough to be a mister," he corrected his new employee, with a kind smile. "How can I help?"

"He's back again."

Shit.

"I'll handle it." Akash dusted his hands off on his apron and made his way quickly out front. He rubbed his forehead with a sigh of exhaustion when he spotted the familiar figure perusing the various pasties on display. "Did you have a sudden craving for scones, Scottie?"

"Come have a coffee with me?" Scottie asked hopefully. He sounded far less demanding than he had previously, but Akash couldn't help a grunt of annoyance. "Just a coffee, that's all."

Deciding not to risk a fight in his shop, Akash herded the overgrown idiot through the back and out into the alley behind the bakery. His patience hovered dangerously close to the end of its tether. Coffee definitely wasn't on the menu for the two of them.

Akash closed the door behind them and leaned against it with his arms crossed over his chest. "Scottie. I don't know if you've concussed yourself one too many times, if you're hard of hearing, or if you truly can't be bothered to listen to what someone tells you. So, I'll say it one last time. I've no interest in sharing coffee, air, or a bed with you."

Scottie opened his mouth, only to immediately snap it shut. His face slowly flushed red. "Why the fuck not?"

Akash resisted the urge to throw his arms up in pure frustration. "Does the reason matter when the answer remains the same? I'm not sodding interested."

For all his bluster, Scottie seemed genuinely astounded by his response. Akash waited to see if he had anything else to say. He didn't.

He just stood and frowned.

"Well?" Akash didn't know what Scottie expected from him. "Why not find someone who is interested in you? Also, maybe don't be a total arsehole to them while you're trying to ask them out. You'll also want to remember no means no. And perhaps less of the scowling?"

Awkward silence followed for an agonizingly long minute. It felt like an hour. *What the hell is he standing there for? Go away, you massive twat.* Akash waited a little more before finally snapping his fingers in front of Scottie to break him out of his daze.

"What?"

"Go home, Scottie. Go home and leave me the hell alone." Akash dragged his fingers roughly through his hair. "I'm not certain what it is you're so desperate to find, but it's not me."

"I—"

Akash slammed the palm of his hand against the door to cut him off. "So help me, Scottie. I'm not warning you off again.

Maybe we can be friends at some point, but right now I'm more likely to kick your arse than shake your hand. Fuck off with yourself."

Returning to the bakery, Akash sent a text to both BC and Taine. They'd take Scottie in hand. If they didn't, he'd follow through on his promise to demonstrate all he'd learned in aikido and Krav Maga.

Daft twit.

BC: Oi. Why do I have to deal with Scottie? It's not my turn.

Akash: He's your friend. Your problem. Stop whining, I'm not Graham, I don't have to put up with it.

BC: Bastard.

Akash: Just sort him out. There's a decent bloke somewhere underneath all the shit.

BC: Yeah, yeah. You owe me pasties.

Akash: For what?

BC: Being fabulous.

Akash: Go annoy Graham.

CHAPTER TWENTY-NINE

HAMISH

The days before a mission rarely dragged by for Hamish. He spent them planning out every detail, prepping gear, and handling last-minute issues. His years of military service had taught him the importance double- and triple-checking before leaving.

For three weeks, Hamish focused on two important tasks to the exclusion just about everything else. He threw himself into physical therapy and managed, to the surprise of his doctor and therapist, to get his shoulder to a satisfactory level of healing. It wouldn't be an issue in the field.

Thank God for the Ross stubbornness.

His second focus was Akash. He wanted a catalogue of memories to choose from in Syria. His days might be exhaustingly busy, but the nights would be lonely with only his thoughts to keep him company.

With his flight early the following morning, Hamish drove over to the bakery to pick his lover up. They wanted to spend the last night together. Akash would drop him off at the airport to keep Hamish from having to park his vehicle there for five months.

Hamish waited until Akash climbed into the vehicle to hold out his closed fist. "I've a present for you."

Akash tossed his bag on the back seat and glanced at the keys dangling in front of his face. "Key to your heart? Bit bulky."

"Don't be an arse." Hamish dropped the set into Akash's hand. "One is for my flat, one is for my Mercedes. You can use my vehicle if you like until I get home. I wanted you to have access if...."

The ever unspoken "if" had haunted them for three weeks. Hamish went out of his way to avoid thinking the worst. He remembered as if it were yesterday the words his instructor drilled into him during training. "Don't predict the future. Plan for every possibility. Don't shit your pants when the bullets start flying."

The dangerous situation in Syria challenged any peacekeeping or aid mission. None of their crew underestimated the potential risk. They'd stand between the doctors and danger.

Giving Akash a key signalled a high level of trust. Hamish never offered easy access to his home to anyone, not even his close friends. He didn't know how to adequately express all of it to the confused baker sitting beside him.

Akash eventually pocketed the keys and dropped his hand to Hamish's thigh. "Ready for a laugh?"

No.

Hamish was anxious for anything to change the subject, so he nodded. Akash surprised him by twisting around to reach into the bag on the back seat. He sat back and revealed a set of keys of his own. "What?"

"I had these made for you—for my flat and bakery. They've been burning a hole in my pocket for a week." Akash gave him a sheepish grin. "Great minds?"

Unable to resist, Hamish grabbed Akash and dragged him across the console until he was partially resting between him and the steering wheel. He grazed their lips together in a teasingly chaste touch. His fingers gripped the baker's shirt to hold him up so they could deepen the kiss.

They tasted each other, tongues delving deeper, hungry for more. Hamish raked his free hand down Akash's shirt front to settle on top of his trousers. He tugged the zipper down and snaked his hand inside to grasp Akash firmly by his already hardening shaft.

Thankful for both the dark interior of his vehicle and the lack of CCTV cameras at the back of the bakery, Hamish stroked Akash firmly and steadily. Their kisses sizzled increasingly out of control.

"Not—" Akash cut himself off midsentence, clutching at Hamish while his hips bucked wildly in the cramped space of the vehicle. He pressed his face into Hamish's chest, biting down in an apparent effort to muffle the sounds of his pleasure.

"Evil. You're evil."

"You're welcome." Hamish waited until his lover caught his breath before helping him sit back up. "Ready for supper?"

"If you think I'm not running upstairs to change, you've got another thing coming." Akash scowled at him. "I'll only be a moment."

Deciding not to leave him alone, Hamish locked up his vehicle and raced up to after him into the flat above the bakery. He wound up taking Akash against the bedroom wall. They eventually made it back downstairs, fully clothed and ready for supper—an hour later than intended.

While Akash divvied up the takeaway they'd stopped for, Hamish set his mind to last-minute packing. He methodically went through his checklists. Once overseas, replacing anything he missed would be nearly impossible.

"Here." Akash handed over a bowl of the noodles from Kaya's Kitchen. He sat cross-legged on the edge of the bed with his own dish. His eyes focused on the open bag on the floor. "Why is this harder than your trip to Sudan?"

Hamish clutched the bowl in one hand, moving to sit beside him. "I've no idea."

Akash played absently with his noodles, hardly taking more than a bite. "It is harder, isn't it?"

"Five months will go by in a twinkling," he promised.

In truth, time tended to fly by on a job. Hamish usually found the stress and intensity pushed things into fast-forward. He imagined for Akash it would feel the exact opposite.

Hamish took both of their bowls and set them on top of the wardrobe. He rested his hands on the wooden surface, and tried to wrap his mind around how to express himself. "You're right. Leaving for Juba didn't weigh on me like tomorrow does."

Akash came up to wind his arms around him and rest his head against Hamish's back. "Let's eat. As you'll remember all of this, I'd rather not mope about for the entire evening."

Nodding his agreement, Hamish squeezed Akash's hands before extracting himself from his embrace. Bowls in hand, they distracted themselves with a movie. He managed to finish up his packing, leaving the bags by the door.

They fell into bed well after midnight. Akash burrowed into his arms with his head resting on Hamish's chest. The baker drifted off into a restless sleep. Hamish didn't sleep for even a second.

He couldn't.

Tightening his hold on Akash, Hamish watched the rise and fall of his chest while he slept. He had finished his letter two days ago. Though he'd known Nye longer, it had been left in Gray's capable hands instead.

Nye would poke and prod at Hamish over it. He'd likely tell Shanti, who would inevitably tease her brother over it. The two brought out the playfulness in each other in a way that frustrated Hamish.

On the other hand, Gray was one of the sternest, grumpiest bastards that he'd ever met, not surprising for a former drill instructor. Hamish trusted the man to treat his farewell letter with respect. *And without the teasing.*

"If you think any harder, you'll break something important." Akash shifted up slightly so his head rested against the crook of Hamish's neck. "Shouldn't you be well-rested for your travels?"

"Ideally."

"Well?" Akash yawned drowsily.

How the hell do I say I'm going to miss you and I'm sodding terrified I won't come home to see where this might've gone between us?

Hamish contemplated using sex as a distraction, anything to avoid his innermost thoughts that he hadn't found the words to express yet. He didn't want to throw a moment away because of fear. "Mentally preparing myself for the next five months."

Weak.

That's so damn weak.

What am I doing?

Hamish grabbed Akash and rolled over until he lay over him, pressing his lover into the sheets. He rested one hand along his collarbone as his other got lost in the mop of dark hair. "You are a complication. A distraction. I'm leaving you here with half of my heart. How the hell am I going to do my job when my mind is filled with exquisite memories of you in my bed?"

Akash raised his hand to rub his thumb across Hamish's lip. "I've no idea if this is a happy revelation or if you're hacked off at me."

"It's a brilliant and inconvenient one." He bit the thumb that was toying with his lip lightly. "I—"

Akash covered his mouth fully with his hand to cut Hamish off. "Don't. Save it. No confessions the night before you leave. If you feel the same in five months, tell me when I meet you at the airport."

His unspoken plea reverberated around them.

Come home to me alive.

CHAPTER THIRTY

AKASH

One month faded into the next for Akash. It seemed as if the holiday decorations had just come down, but the calendar told him three months had passed. His mood sunk deeper with each passing week.

The distance was hard. Akash realised he'd found a place of comfort with Hamish. Email and dodgy Skype connections barely knocked the edge off.

His friends dragged him out at least once a week, his parents insisted on family dinners every other weekend though the drive about killed him, and Wyatt or Gray stopped by the bakery frequently. None of it seemed out of the ordinary. Yet, all of it felt like a conspiracy to distract him from worrying.

How the bloody hell am I not going to stress?

Syria had all but imploded. Bombings had increased exponentially over the last two months. Any sort of medical facility was usually skirted around by combatants, yet the news covered multiple stories of hospitals either completely or partially destroyed.

Akash held his breath through every report. Never before in his life had he actually sat each morning to watch the news and read the paper. Freddie insisted it was bad for his health, but he couldn't stop.

What if he dies? What if I'm not watching the news and he dies? How the hell does anyone handle long-distance relationships? This is total shit.

His fear occasionally bordered on hysterical and irrational. Akash appreciated Freddie's constant attempts to bring him back to real world. He wished it helped.

Shanti: Nye and I are going to the Sin Bin tonight. Want to come?

Akash: No.

Shanti: Please?

Akash: No.

Shanti: Aki.

Akash: I'm tired. It's been an exhausting day. I've zero interest in drinking, dancing, or listening to loud music. Enjoy yourself.

Do I have "depressed" tattooed on my forehead?

Closing up shop, Akash decided to head over to Hamish's flat. He spent at least one or two nights a week there and usually drove his lover's vehicle. Checking on Ganesh first, he made his way out the back where the Mercedes was parked.

He barely resisted the urge to inhale the scent of the vehicle. Sitting in the driver's seat, he could almost imagine Hamish's arms around him. He'd definitely fallen hard.

I'm pathetic.

I'm living in a romantic tragedy, and I'm pathetic.

"You closed early."

Akash peered around the front of the SUV to find Gray sitting on his Harley, leaning forward against the handlebars. "Something wrong?"

Gray shook his head with a gravelly chuckle. "You're going to want to remember how to breathe. It won't do your man a bit of good if you wind up having a heart attack while he's gone."

"Did you want something?" Akash couldn't endure a lecture from anyone else on how he shouldn't worry.

"He wrote you a letter." Gray twisted the heavy ring on his finger absently. "We all write them if we've got folks left at home. People that we love. I haven't written one in years. Can't be bothered. Hamish wrote only one, and it's got your name on it."

"I—"

Gray held up a hand to stop him from moving forward. "Not giving it to you. I wouldn't betray his faith in me. Just trust he fucking cared enough to bare his fucking soul to you."

He ran his fingers tiredly through his hair, making more of a mess of it than an entire day of work had done. "Why even mention it if you won't let me read it?"

"Stop fucking moping around like he's already dead." Gray kicked his bike into gear and walked it slowly forward.

"Sleeping in his bed won't bring him home."

"Has anyone ever told you what an arse you are?" Akash glared at the man, who managed to glare and smirk at the same time. *Impressive.*

"Every fucking day." Gray winked at him. "You're fucking welcome."

Arsehole. Maybe that's why I've seen him and Scottie together. Arses of a feather flock together.

The rumble of the Harley drowned out any response Akash wanted to make. Gray nodded once in acknowledgement before riding off. *Honestly.* He could admit, at least to himself, that the man had a point.

He drove over to Hamish's flat with one question on his mind. What was in the letter? It started as curiosity, but slowly morphed into a different sort of sadness.

How do you write a goodbye note just in case you might die?

His respect for those who served in the military went even higher. Akash reached out to the one person he could always trust to be brutally honest with him—his father. His dad asked to call him back later in the evening.

Akash showered, ate supper, and had just gotten comfortable in front of the telly when his mobile rang. "Papa?"

"Sorry. Your mum wouldn't understand part of this." His father's voice soothed his fears, as it always did. "So, your Hamish wrote a letter."

"Apparently."

"I wrote your mum one." His dad paused for several seconds, clearing his throat loudly. "Hardest thing I've ever done. Imagining not coming home to her. I don't know about Hamish, but I couldn't write the truth without placing myself in the darkest emotional space I can imagine. Broke my heart. I burned it in a bonfire when I finally retired from service."

"Should I tell him I know?" Akash had considered texting Hamish before opting to reach out to his father first.

"Don't."

Silence.

"Don't," his father repeated seriously. "He needs to know you're safe. Ask him when he's home. Not now."

"You're right." Akash hated to admit it because his innate curiosity made it hard to resist, but he would. "Thanks, Papa."

"Akash?" His father didn't wait for his response. "This boy—he loves you."

What the…?

"We haven't exactly said." Akash tried to disappear into the sofa. "I'm pathetic."

"You're not pathetic. And whether the words left his lips or not, the man clearly loves you." His father shot his truth like an arrow straight through Akash's denial. "Do you love him?"

"I don't know."

"Stop biting your lip. It's a sure sign you're lying. I don't even have to see you to know you're doing it." His father chuckled when Akash cursed under his breath. "Your mum's calling for me. Come for dinner this weekend. We miss you. We love you. Don't ask him about the letter."

Akash stared at his mobile when the call disconnected. "Right. *Parents.*"

His evening took a turn toward the bizarre with a text

from Scottie, who apologised for being a "boorish twat." The message included a promise not to badger him for a date again. It ended with a hope they could eventually become friends.

How incredibly extraordinary.

Had Scottie hit his head on something? Suffered a personality change? What in the world had provoked him into saying sorry?

Glancing toward the window to check for flying pigs, Akash opted to accept the apology and ignore the offer of friendship for the time being. He preferred to see if Scottie's actions proved his words to be true or not. Cordial was something they could both manage without much effort.

A check of his watch informed him Hamish was probably still awake. Akash sent a quick hello text. He stretched out on the couch, getting comfortable to wait for a response. He'd almost drifted off to sleep when his mobile buzzed.

Hamish: Still awake?

Akash: Barely.

Hamish: Sounds like your day has been as long as mine.

Akash: I imagine yours has been worse.

Akash: Two months feel like a century to wait. I've run out of ways to say I miss you.

Hamish: I've better ways—but you were quite insistent on my waiting.

Akash: I meant it.

Hamish: Fuck. I've got to go. Don't watch the news. It'll make you stress. You know the thing I can't tell you? Pretend I've already said it.

Akash: Be safe.

Akash immediately turned on the news and grabbed his laptop to open multiple tabs to five different sources. He wouldn't sleep. He couldn't until Hamish texted him to say they'd returned safely to where their temporary home was set up.

Gods.

Keep them all safe. I can't lose him now.

CHAPTER THIRTY-ONE

HAMISH

From: HamishRoss@HRSP.co.uk
Date: Monday, 02 April, 2018 at 05:45:27 +0200
To: akash@robinsonbakery.co.uk
Subject: Early morning thoughts.

I've a brief moment to myself this morning, which won't last long, I know. We'll be heading home in a little over a week. I'm honestly stunned we've had no injuries thus far. It's a miracle.

Sleeping on a cot brings me back to

```
my first months of military service.
It's as shit now as it was then.
   I want to be home.
   I want you in my bed.
   I wouldn't say no to one of your
pasties, either.
   Wish you'd let me say the words.
   Hamish
```

Syria proved as chaotic and dangerous as expected. Hamish made a ritual of reminding the others daily their job was to help the medical staff only. They weren't peacekeepers or active duty military. They couldn't engage combatants.

Days went by slowly in a slog of rescuing civilians buried in their own homes. It was the hell of war. Hamish had always hoped his tours in Afghanistan were the last he'd see of it.

Hamish saw nothing but pain and suffering in the eyes of the people they helped. Half of the time, they ended up working with the White Helmets, volunteers who worked as first responders in the battered cities. He admired their courage in the face of such abject misery and constant danger.

They had almost no respite, barely had time to remember to breathe. Akash emailed him frequently with updates on the goings-on in Cardiff, or sometimes just to say hello. Hamish read them over repeatedly, happy for any connection with his baker.

April had been a busy month for both of them. The arson investigation had finally closed with a surprise ending. A second fire less than a few hundred yards from the bakery caught the detectives' attention. They were able to connect both incidents, along with three others, apprehending a serial arsonist in the process.

It turned out the twins' stepfather hadn't been directly involved. Marc had messaged him a news article on the fires. The arsonist confessed to over thirty fires dating back ten years; he claimed to have heard a man in a pub going on about the bakery and decided to make it his next target.

We can't exactly arrest him for an overheard conversation. Convenient for the stepfather.

It was at least a weight off his shoulders. Hamish had worried that someone might be wandering around Cardiff, a danger to Akash. He knew his lover had the ability to take care of himself, but he still worried.

On the heels of the arrest, Akash told him the twins had ended up facing their abuser at trial anyway. They'd been brave. Terrified, but extremely courageous. The two would hopefully be free of his torment for a while at least, given the sentence and restraining order handed out to him.

He made a mental note to ask Gray or Wyatt to check up on the situation. Either would be a good choice for intimidating the man. Alice and Alex might finally find healing.

God, I miss Akash.

Skype hadn't worked for them in two weeks. Internet wasn't exactly reliable with almost daily bombings. It seemed more important to reserve their satellite connection for emergency communications.

Under all of his complaints, Hamish knew it boiled down to him missing Akash. They only had a week or so left to go. They'd survived months and months, a week would be nothing at all.

"It's getting worse." Adam—Hamish refused to call a grown man Scorch—perched on the cot across from his. "Another hospital was hit in the south of the city last night."

"I'm aware." Hamish sighed. "It's a shitshow, and we've no authority to do anything other than help with the bodies. An effort in futility."

Vinnie joined them with three brimming cups of coffee. He carefully handed two of them over, keeping one for himself. "We've a bigger issue, as the planes have been straying closer towards us."

"I've noticed." Hamish had discussed it at length with the lead doctor, who agreed with his assessment of the danger but refused to take his advice on moving into consideration. "We'll do what we can."

"So, nothing but fucking hope we don't get blown to fucking bits." Cole, or Voodoo as Wyatt preferred to call him, strode into the room with his own mug of coffee. "Doctor wants to get a move on."

"We've a week left." Hamish quaffed down the lukewarm coffee and set the cup aside. "All we can do is try to save as many as possible while keeping our arses out of the fire."

"Easier said than done." Cole exchanged a glance with his fellow American, who shrugged. "Chug your coffee. Say a prayer to the god of war that he doesn't abandon us."

Walking out of the building they used as a bunk, Hamish stared up at the cloudless sky. Plumes of smoke were visible in the distance. *Closer than yesterday.* He rubbed the back of his neck when the hairs suddenly stood on end.

"Oi. Hamster." Vinnie jogged up behind him. He nodded toward the small bit of the horizon they could see through the few buildings still standing. "We should let the doctors know."

Hamish had never been much of a praying man, but couldn't help sending one up anyway. "Shit."

He had a bad feeling. From the glances sent his way, the others harboured similar worries. His eyes stayed on the skies, and he sent up a prayer to the gods of war to spare them for another week.

It was selfish. More than anything else, Hamish wanted to make it home to Akash. He'd seen so many hearts broken by a loved one never returning. *Please don't let me be the next one on the list. I'm not ready.*

Akash, if I don't make it back to say this, I'll send it into the ether and hope you hear me anyway. I love you.

I love you.

I hope I sodding make it home to say it in person.

CHAPTER THIRTY-TWO

AKASH

A storm had rolled into Cardiff, refusing to leave and putting Akash on edge. The hairs on the back of his neck stood up with the first flash of lighting. Never prone to superstition, he still considered staying indoors until the skies cleared.

Six in the morning. C'mon, Akash, you've got scones to make. Get up.

Sparing a glance for his laptop, Akash decided to get an early start on his morning. Hamish usually only messaged him in the evening. He hated scrolling through his emails and not seeing anything from the man.

Seven.

The kitchen was covered in the chaotic energy he lived to create. He had dough proving on the side, in the fridge, and the freezer. Three trays were already in the ovens. His morning assistant had arrived to help, only to find he'd done all of their work.

Eight.

With his assistant manning the front, Akash continued to force his mind to focus on flour, spices, and the science of baking. It kept him from dwelling on whatever had his nerves on edge. He stayed far away from the news, preferring not to know if the worst had happened.

Nine.

"That American bloke's out here for you."

Akash paused in the midst of kneading one last batch of dough for the morning. "Which one?"

"The one that doesn't have a Harley-Davidson."

He'd caught the young university student drooling over Gray's motorbike several times. "Send Wyatt in here. I've got another twenty minutes of this to do."

"Akash?"

He paused briefly in the process of slamming the dough on the work bench to find Wyatt without his normal smile. "No. No. *No.* You're not swanning into my shop looking as if the world has ended. I won't have it. You can take your Yankee arse right out the door and come back with good news."

Wyatt held up a hand to try and get him to listen. "A bomb—"

"Don't." Akash twisted violently away from him, trying to block the words with his body. If he didn't hear it, everything would still be completely fine. "Don't."

"Akash." Wyatt didn't try to approach him, wisely staying

across the kitchen with the various tables separating them. "Akash?"

He gripped the counter in front of him, bending forward with his head down and eyes closed. He breathed slowly through a sudden wave of nausea, and he knew the truth had to be heard. "Go on, then."

Wyatt was silent long enough that Akash turned back around to face him. He gazed searchingly at Akash before finally getting on with it. "We've reports from Syria. A hospital in their area was hit this morning. Hospital is a generous term for the cobbled-together medical facility, but nonetheless, a bomb struck and fucking levelled it to the ground."

"And Hamish?"

"No idea." Wyatt shrugged helplessly, looking like he felt as impotent as Akash did. "We've tried every fucking way we know how to reach them. Nothing. Either their equipment has been destroyed, or...."

Or they've been destroyed.

No.

He's not allowed to die on me.

Not now.

The unspoken, likely possibility dropped Akash to his knees. He'd disregarded his father's insights into the depth of his feelings towards Hamish. The chasm of grief in his soul proved his denials to be the massive lie they were.

Leaning forward with his hands flat on the floor, Akash slammed them into the ground several times. He balled his hands up into fists and tried to remember how to control himself. With his eyes closed tightly against tears, his breathing slowly regulated until he could at least pretend some semblance of normalcy.

Shifting off his knees, Akash sat with his back to one of the many cupboard doors in his kitchen. He covered his face with his hands, regretting his decision to keep Hamish from saying three stupid words that he'd never hear now. *I'm a sodding fool, and I'm going to pay for it.*

"We can't give up on them yet." Wyatt crouched beside him and rested a hand tentatively on his shoulder. "The Hamster's resilient."

Resilient.

Not immortal.

Akash tilted his head until it hit the cupboard. He brought his hand to rub at his chest to ease the tightening there. "When will you know anything?"

"You'll be the first to know," Wyatt answered without actually answering, something Akash had noticed both he and Hamish were particularly skilled at. "Don't lose hope yet."

Getting to his feet, Akash found his body moved like he was stuck in a vat of treacle while washing his hands clean. He grabbed absently at the ball of dough on the table. His fingers dug into it, while he smiled dully at Wyatt.

"Pies won't make themselves," he muttered dismissively.

Studiously ignoring Wyatt's attempts to comfort him, Akash focused on the sticky and ruined mess of water and flour. He knew the dough wouldn't be good for dog biscuits, let alone delicate pastry. If he didn't give himself something to do, he worried the weight of grief would drown him.

"One of us will stop by later this evening to give you

an update." Wyatt dropped a hand on his shoulder to squeeze it. "Nye's been on the phone with your sister. He said she'd mentioned stopping in to see you."

Shit.

It was lunchtime when Shanti came for a visit. Akash found himself stuck in the middle of a massive order for his curried fruit and cream cheese pastries. She'd given up badgering him and left him to his work.

Thank the gods of baking for my brief reprieve.

His mobile had buzzed almost nonstop with concerned messages from friends wanting to know if he'd seen the reports on the news. After his younger sister's visit came ones from Aled, Jack, and Freddie.

He appreciated the concern.

He just wanted them to bugger off and leave him to his thoughts.

Closing up shop two hours early, Akash trudged up the stairs to his flat. He collapsed on the couch and buried his face in a cushion. Tears refused to come; they clogged up his throat instead, threatening to choke him.

An hour into his morose vigil, Alice and Alex used their key to his flat. They sat on either side of him, not saying a word. He gave a watery chuckle when Alice pushed her comfort stim, a soft otter plush, into his arms.

The twins had an immense gift at remaining comfortable with silence for long periods. Akash found comfort in it. He was grateful for their showing concern in the best way they knew.

The knock came five minutes until midnight. Akash

returned the otter to Alice. He sternly forced himself to his feet and over to the door.

Akash blinked in surprise, as he'd expected to see a completely different American. "Gray?"

Without saying a word, the man shoved a plain envelope into his hands. Akash assumed the worst had been confirmed. Crushing the letter in his hands, he collapsed as Gray rushed forward to catch him.

"Hey, fuck, listen, we don't know yet. I thought you should read this—keep your spirits up." Gray kept Akash on his feet, waiting for him to regain some semblance of control over his own limbs. "I see why Earp said not to give it to you yet. Aren't you Brits supposed to have stiff upper lips?"

"Scaring the shit out of me is how you keep my spirits up?" Akash pulled away to berate the man only to find an approving gleam in his eyes. "Don't be an arse."

"Comes naturally." Gray released him, nodding toward the crushed envelope Akash clutched in his fist. "Read it, but don't give up just yet. We're a stubborn breed. I think the Hamster will surprise you."

If the worst happens, I love you. Don't doubt it, if I never found the courage to say the words. Seemed too soon. Is it ever too soon? I'd so many dreams about where our relationship might go. Seems a waste to imagine it not happening.

I'd have loved you until age took us away from each

other, I think.

I wanted the chance to see if I was right.

Now, it's too late, if you're reading this. I'm sorry I waited too long to tell you.

Love,
Hamish

With painstaking care, Akash flattened out the crumpled letter. He tried to erase the lines caused from his crumpling it into a ball. Hamish's last words to him had to hold him through whatever might happen in the next few days and months.

"Akash?" Alice hesitated by the door of his bedroom, where he'd gone to read in privacy. "Your phone keeps buzzing. Mr Baird's is as well. He went outside to talk, though."

Sodding hell on earth.

This is it.

This could be the worst news imaginable.

Akash dropped the letter to avoid crushing it for the second time. "Just need to use the loo. I'll check my phone in a moment."

Never. Never touching my sodding phone again. He can't be…. I can't. Shit.

CHAPTER THIRTY-THREE

AKASH

If one more arsehole knocks on my door, I'll shove them down the stairs.

His friends and family went from ringing him at all hours to showing up at his flat. Akash had no idea what they expected to find or how they hoped to help. He wished they'd all leave him alone to process and to grieve.

Not that I know if I've anything to mourn, at least not officially.

Forty-eight hours seemed a lifetime. Akash dragged himself forcibly through his daily routine. His shop wouldn't run itself.

The letter stayed in his pocket. Akash was afraid to leave it anywhere. He hadn't eaten all day—barely remembered to feed the cat.

Five minutes before closing, the jingle sounded the arrival of a late customer. Akash stood up from where he'd already started to clean out one of the displays. He dropped the platter in his hands, completely ignoring the explosion of glass at his feet.

Hamish stood before him with a slight smile, cuts and bruises evident on his face and his arm in a sling once again. "Hello."

So, not actually dead.

Brilliant.

Don't pass out on the broken glass and die.

Oh my God. Oh my God. Oh my God.

He's not dead.

"Hi." Akash hopped over the display case and landed a few feet away from his battered but blissfully alive lover. "Hi."

Oh for fuck's sake, say something else, you moron.

Hamish inched closer to him, bringing his relatively uninjured arm up and resting his palm against Akash's chest. His fingers tightened on his apron as he used it to drag him over. "I'm so sorry I worried you."

Akash wanted to punch the man for the sheer idiocy of his apology. He wrapped his arms around Hamish's waist, loosening his hold when the man grunted in pain. "Sorry? You're sorry? I thought you died. Died. Not-coming-back died."

"Aki. *Aki.* Have you heard?" Shanti dashed into the bakery with Nye following close behind. She stopped in her tracks when Akash eased himself away from Hamish. "Oh.

He's already here."

"I noticed." He laughed a little hysterically. "If this is some bizarre dream that I'm going to wake up from, I will be truly hacked off at the lot of you."

Shanti caught Hamish by the sleeve and nudged him back toward Akash. "Why don't you two go upstairs? Nye can help me close up shop."

"I can?" Nye smirked at her and dodged the smack on his arm. "Go on. We'll keep anyone else who shows up at bay."

Knowing they'd eventually be inundated by friends, Akash warned his sister about the glass before leading Hamish through the bakery and up the stairs into his flat. He belatedly remembered the complete disaster it was. In a rare show of temper, he'd practically wrecked his living room in the middle of the night, when his grief become too much to handle.

He went to pick up an overturned chair, only to pause when Hamish placed a hand on his. "Thought you died."

"I know."

"Thought you fucking died on me," Akash whispered bitterly.

"I *know*."

"Thought you sodding died." Akash dragged his sleeve roughly across his eyes. "I haven't slept much or eaten. Couldn't. I kept seeing you buried under some building."

"I'm sorry." Hamish tugged on his hand, but Akash wasn't ready to be held. "Shall I tell you about it?"

With a sharp nod and a ragged sigh, Akash swiped the mess from the sofa. He fell into a seat as his legs lost the ability to hold him up. Hamish came over to sit beside him, and after a brief hesitation rested his hand on his lover's thigh.

Akash couldn't keep his eyes off his hand; it was covered in cuts and scratches. "You're not dead."

"No." Hamish sank slowly back into the cushions with a pained groan. "None of us made it out completely unscathed."

Deciding tea would be required, Akash made a pot of one of his favourite blends. He listened to Hamish's tale while preparing two cups for them. The further the story went, the more he regretted not grabbing a large bottle of wine instead.

It seemed the daily bombings in Syria had crept closer and closer to them, until the moment they feared happened, a catastrophic hit on the makeshift hospital that all but flattened the partially damaged buildings. They'd been lucky.

Lucky?

Out of the doctors, nurses, patients, and security team, they'd suffered only three fatalities—all medical staff. Hamish choked up a little when he spoke of hunting through the rubble for Vinnie, who'd been inside at the time. He'd dug through the debris, which had been the cause of almost all of his own injuries, to find his friend.

Akash was out of his depth when it came to offering comfort. He decided the only thing to do was listen. Even so, Hamish didn't say much about the attack itself, and eventually fell silent altogether.

It reminded Akash of a conversation from his youth. After watching an action movie, he'd been flush with excitement, wanting to hear all about his dad's experiences in the military. His father had taught him a lesson about asking questions when one wasn't prepared to hear the answers.

Hamish drained his tea and set his cup on the coffee table. He picked up a shredded envelope to stare at it. "I'll be giving a certain American a swift kick in the bollocks the next time I see him."

"No, you really won't." Akash reached into his pocket to pull out the letter. Ganesh had claimed the envelope as his own personal toy. "In my mind, you were dead, and these words were all I had left."

"Not much to hold on to." Hamish plucked the paper out of his hands. "I'm not much of a wordsmith."

All the dancing around the unspoken words pushed him to the brink of losing what little he had left of his emotional patience. Akash flung his empty cup absently toward the coffee table, and practically leapt at Hamish. He straddled his lover's legs and gripped him firmly by the front of his shirt.

"Aki?" Hamish shifted slightly to adjust his injured arm, and wrapped his other one around Akash, likely to keep him from tumbling to the floor. "Something wrong?"

"I thought you fucking died." He forgot all about Hamish's injuries, shaking the man by his shirt to punctuate each word. "And the only way I knew you might love me came from a piece of paper."

Hamish pressed him even closer. "I love you."

CHAPTER THIRTY-FOUR

HAMISH

As the rush of energy disappeared, Akash all but passed out on the couch asleep. Hamish barely managed to get him up and through the obstacles in the living room into his bedroom. He wondered if the man had slept at all in two days.

I haven't, not much.

Not at all.

Fully dressed with a sling didn't make for the most comfortable sleeping arrangements. Hamish didn't mind. Akash slept peacefully beside him; he'd suffer through almost anything for the peace it brought him.

It had been a hell of a few days. When everything around them stabilized after the bombings stopped, none of them knew if they'd lost anyone. Hamish had been the furthest away, still in a meeting with several of the doctors.

For several awful minutes, Hamish hadn't known if any of them would be returning to Cardiff. Vinnie had had the closest brush with death. He'd been found using his body to shield a six-year-old patient.

The situation was made worse by their inability to reach out to anyone. It had taken a miracle and a few favours to get all of them out of the country. Vinnie had required immediate medical attention for internal injuries, but thankfully would make a full recovery.

Two of the doctors and one nurse they'd promised to protect hadn't been so lucky. Hamish closed his eyes against the rush of emotion. He hated to fail.

And I failed them.

Logically, Hamish knew without a doubt that nothing outside of moving the entire facility would've changed the outcome of the day. He'd argued for it and been shut down. So instead of following his instincts, he'd done his best to protect them within the scope of what the doctors wanted.

"Are you hungry?" Akash rolled over onto his back with a tired groan. "What time is it?"

"A quarter to three in the morning." Hamish had barely managed five minutes of dozing. "You should be sleeping. And you *never* responded to my declaration."

"Consider it your punishment for scaring me half to death." Akash smiled tiredly at him when Hamish nudged him with his elbow. "I distinctly recall you telling me not to hand over my heart. Are you certain you deserve it?"

"*Aki.*"

Akash sat up slowly with a yawn. He leaned over Hamish to get a look at his clock on the nightstand. "Almost three. Want a fry-up?"

"No, well, yes, I'd love one. But first, I want you to say you love me." Hamish grabbed Akash with his uninjured hand to yank him closer. He kissed him, their first in what seemed like ages. "Do you?"

"Yes, Hamish, you daft idiot. I love you—but I haven't eaten much since you decided to almost get blown up. So at the moment, my adoration for you is tied with how I feel about food." Akash brushed his lips lightly and playfully against Hamish's. "Let's have a midnight snack."

Their midnight snack turned into a more substantial meal. Hamish had spotted ingredients for chicken curry, and Akash caved to his urge for comfort food. He dragged a chair over so he could watch his lover in comfort.

Stretching his legs out in front of him, Hamish found himself getting misty-eyed out of nowhere. *How domestic we are. How comfortable.* Akash tossed him a piece of potato before dumping the rest into the pan.

They ate. The warmth of the curry soothed some of the raw edges of their nerves. Akash drifted off to sleep not long after they returned to bed. Hamish remained awake long enough to send a text to Wyatt.

Hamish: You check on Vinnie?

Wyatt: You're lucky I got up early. Why the fuck are you up at five in the morning?

Hamish: Trouble sleeping.

Wyatt: Vinnie's in intensive care, or whatever you call

it here. He's in good hands. Lily's going to check in on him. When everyone's recovered, we're going to have a long chat about the contracts we take.

Hamish: Aled?

Wyatt: Yes, my husband did have a very long chat with me, several of them. Go to sleep, Hamster. What happened wasn't your fault.

Hamish: Taking the day off.

Wyatt: You're taking the next fucking week off.

On the whole, Hamish had always believed any situation could be made secure if they had total control over decisions being made in the field. He intended to evaluate the wording of their contracts going forward. Clients couldn't be allowed to completely dictate their security.

The misadventure in Syria had also brought one thing into focus for Hamish. *I am in love with Akash. He's the one.* He turned his mind to what he felt was the obvious next step for them.

Will he marry me?

Hamish sank down on the bed with a tired groan. He smiled when Akash rolled over to rest his head on his chest, throwing an arm across him. "Rest well, Aki."

God.

I hope he says yes.

CHAPTER THIRTY-FIVE

AKASH

Akash shot up in bed with a panicked shout. He flailed for a second when a hand clamped down on his arm. *Shit.* "You're not dead."

"No." Hamish had obviously stripped down to his boxers before going to sleep. He watched in silence when Akash bent closer to inspect the bruises, nicks, and abrasions on his upper body. "Might have a few new scars."

Akash glanced up to find the same faraway gaze in Hamish's eyes from the previous night. "No new names for your tattoo, though?"

He breathed out deeply and shook his head. "Not this time."

When Hamish closed his eyes, Akash decided it was time

to let the conversation go. He wanted to help in some way. An arm came around him and drew him down against his lover's body; an early morning doze was apparently on the schedule.

"When do you have to get up to open the bakery?" Hamish asked gruffly, breaking the comfortable but weighted silence between them. "Soon, I imagine."

Akash knew he should've been up hours ago. "It'll keep."

"Help me shower?" Hamish ran his fingers through Akash's mussed hair. He played with the ends. "Think I'm developing a fetish for your hair."

"As long as you don't attempt to take it from me, I'm fine with it." Akash rolled away from him when Hamish yanked at his hair. "Let's get you in the shower, Major."

"Retired."

Akash pinned him with a pointed stare. "Right. Is that why you introduced yourself to my parents as Major Hamish Ross?"

"First impressions." He appeared the picture of innocence. "I thought about you after the chaos had settled and lives weren't on the line."

"Oh?" Akash froze in the middle of getting out of the bed. He sat down on the mattress and waited for elaboration. "Good thoughts?"

Hamish extended his arm until his hand found Akash's, threading their fingers together. "Wonderful thoughts. Flashes of the future really. Ours."

Akash suddenly found himself holding his breath for no reason whatsoever. Where was Hamish going with this conversation? "What did you see?"

Hamish smiled teasingly at him, his dark blue eyes sparkling for the first time since he'd returned. "You'll see."

"Well, if you're done teasing my curiosity into a state of frothing, why don't we take that shower?" Akash had spent years learning to be patient. *How hard can this be? Very.* "Not even a hint?"

"No."

"Arse." Akash stripped out of his clothes and headed toward his bathroom, leaving the chuckling Hamish on the bed. "I'll run a bath. I'm too tired to stand up."

With a tub full of hot sudsy water, Akash climbed in and made space for Hamish to slide in across from him. Their legs spread to fit each other's bodies. His bath didn't quite have the magnificent size of his lover's.

They ran their hand along each other's legs. Akash leaned his head against the tile behind him. He allowed the weight of his worry and pain from the last month to evaporate.

In the abstract, months of Hamish being far away in a dangerous place melted away with his firm caresses. Akash found his mind drifting to thoughts of the future as well. He knew any long-term life with a lover who constantly worked on the knife edge of danger brought with it a certain level of worry.

Is it worth it?

Do I have the strength and heart to carry on when he's doing what he's passionate about?

Akash found his eyes going to the hand running along the inside of his legs. *Aren't my hands as strong? My heart's as sturdy as his. Do I love him or not?* He moved his body slightly and reached for the soap. "Will this hurt all your scrapes and cuts?"

They both sat up, trading the soap back and forth. They soaped every inch of each other's bodies, making gentle love to water-slick skin. Akash paid particular attention to Hamish's hard shaft bobbing in the water; his hands froze for a moment when his lover returned the favour, wrapping his fingers around his erection.

Bending forward and thanking the gods for his flexibility, Akash tilted his head so Hamish could press their lips together. Their tongues languidly explored while their fingers danced over hot and heavy flesh. He wondered if they both longed for release to ease the last weight of worry that had lingered in their minds.

One stroke after the other, Akash enjoyed taking his time. He saw no reason to rush. They'd waited for this for months.

Why hurry to the finish line when the race was delayed for so long?

"Have a condom handy?" Hamish tightened his grip on Akash. "Ride me."

"What about your shoulder?" Akash was all for enjoying himself, but not at the risk of damaging Hamish further.

"More of a precaution than anything. Doesn't feel bad this morning. Hop on, Aki." Hamish moved his hand away. "Can you manage it?"

Getting on his knees, Akash stretched out as far as possible until his fingers snagged the edge of one of the drawers on the cabinet under the sink. He opened it and rooted around blindly for the packet of condoms. With a little cheer of success, he fumbled for a second before getting it open.

"Maybe I should stand up?" Hamish got to his feet only to slip slightly, grabbing at Akash to balance himself. "Or, maybe we should get out of the tub to avoid ending up in emergency?"

Sliding the condom on Hamish, Akash used it to lead Hamish into the bedroom. They left wet footprints on his wooden floor. Ganesh dodged out of the way, disappearing into his favourite hiding space on a mound of blankets on one of the bookshelves.

They played around with different positions. None felt perfect. Hamish finally pushed Akash on his side, sliding up next to him while their arms wound around each other. With their shafts pressed together, they drove each other to a slow-building release.

"Why do we always end up needing two showers?" Akash complained breathlessly. "Always."

"Marry me?"

Akash narrowed his eyes on Hamish. "Are you serious? We're naked, still covered in suds and other things. Now you ask me?"

"More effort required?" Hamish bent his head forward and licked along the crook of Akash's neck. "Can I help you think about it?"

Akash intended to smack the man on the arm and tell him to go have a shower. He didn't mean to lean into his caress. *"Hamish."*

"Aki. Marry me?" Hamish gripped him by the hair, yanking his head back hard. His teeth and tongue worked every inch of

Akash's neck available. "Please?

Should I? Do I want to? Is it too soon? Sod it. It's been less than a year—an intense year.

"Yes." Akash paused before continuing. "You get to tell my parents."

"You're worth it." Hamish gave an exaggerated groan. "No second thoughts?"

"I'm sure we'll both have them when my sister finds out." Akash had no doubts Shanti would take over every single part of the planning if they let her. "Akash Ross? Akash Robinson? Akash Robinson-Ross?"

"What are you doing?"

"Trying to decide who I'm going to be," Akash teased. He dodged away from the fingers that began to tickle him. "Evil."

After cleaning up quickly, Akash grabbed the closest shirt to the bed, which happened to be Hamish's. He wandered into the kitchen to whip up a snack for them. His mobile sat innocently on the counter, taunting and daring him.

A quick mass text to his friends wouldn't hurt anything, would it?

Freddie: Brilliant. Taine says congrats.

Jack: You wanker. Now I'll be completely alone in my state of singleness.

Francis: How lovely. Caddock says you can use the Sin Bin. I've told him to mind his own business and let you two plan your own nuptials.

Graham: Was it mid sex? BC and I have a bet that it was mid sex.

Aled: I won't tell Wyatt. He'll crow about it for ages.

Hamish can be the one to share it with him. I'm so pleased for both of you.

With a roll of his eyes, Akash set his phone aside. Everyone he knew in Cardiff and Cornwall would likely know his news within the next few hours. *Bugger.* He belatedly realised his parents should've been the first to hear about it.

Ah, well.

I'll distract them with wedding plans.

That will work, right?

Shit.

EPILOGUE

HAMISH

After they told Akash's family about the engagement, his lover's youngest sister went into hyperdrive. She wanted to create the perfect wedding for the two of them. Hamish had only a few demands: no flowers, or religious overtones, and a cake worthy of his talented baker.

His initial worry about Shanti going overboard and turning it into a circus didn't pan out at all. She truly hoped to create a memorable day for her only brother, and used all of her contacts in the design world to make it happen. Hamish told Akash that they'd have to find a way to thank her for taking on all the work, leaving them to do nothing but relax and enjoy.

The question of where to get married required three months to answer. Neither of them wanted to waste gobs of cash on a wedding. The problem resolved itself when Scottie brought them an invitation to use the Sin Bin; all the men who owned it had discussed wanting to offer it as their gift to Hamish and Akash.

Scottie had gracefully declined an invitation to the ceremony.

Smart man.

Hamish asked Wyatt to be his best man, while Shanti played best woman for her brother. They hadn't wanted an overly done ceremony. Neither of them was religious, so Nye got himself licensed as a celebrant for a laugh, allowing him to officiate the ceremony.

No flower girls or ring bearers. No ushers. Nothing either he or Akash deemed as unnecessary.

A little over seven months after proposing, December 1st brought with it a beautifully clear and cool winter day for their wedding. They'd slept apart at Shanti's insistence. She wanted their reactions to each other at the ceremony to be genuine.

"Ready to get hitched?" Wyatt followed him into the nightclub. "Not too late to make a run for it."

"How long have you been married now?" Hamish stared pointedly at his friend's wedding band. "Is Aled finally tired of you?"

Any retort Wyatt might've made died on his lips when they stepped into the room that usually held live music concerts. Shanti and her friends had worked incredibly hard to turn it into a space fit for a wedding ceremony. The reception would be held on the dance floor—she'd promised the music would be something they could all enjoy.

Navy blue and gold silk covered the walls. Rows of gold chairs with blue sashes made a circle in the centre of the room, with a black carpet running from the doors down through the middle of the chairs. In less than an hour, Hamish would stand at the end of the path, getting married.

Lights had been strung from the rafters. Hamish noticed his military badge had been embossed on each one. He was touched at the fine details Shanti had obviously gone out of her way to include.

"You clean up nicely." Wyatt stepped over to straighten Hamish's navy blue bow tie. He'd been thrilled to find Shanti's selection for him was a simple black suit with white shirt and the tie. "We both do. I'd fuck us."

Hamish shoved Wyatt away from him. "I will blacken your eye on my wedding day."

"Brits. No sense of fucking humour."

"Yanks. No sense of propriety." Hamish dragged his old friend into a hug. "Thanks for being here."

"Someone has to prop you up when fear kicks in."

"And I suddenly regret not asking someone else." Hamish pushed Wyatt away again, and straightened his suit. "Oh, wonderful, people that aren't you."

Twenty minutes later, Hamish found to his surprise that his nerves had kicked in. Their friends and family had gotten seated while he stood with Wyatt and a grinning Nye. *Hope he hasn't decided to play Rowan Atkinson in* Four Weddings and a Funeral. *I'll kill him. Akash'll bring him back, and then we'll kill him together.* His murderous thoughts evaporated when the doors opened, and Akash strode in with Shanti at his side.

Their wedding attire paid homage to their mother's side of the family. Akash wore a navy blue *sherwani*, and the long silk coat with golden embroidery went perfectly with his dark trousers. Hamish wanted to drag him over by the scarf around his neck and kiss the life out of him.

Maybe after the I do's.

"Don't fucking cry." Wyatt bent forward to whisper to him, grunting when Hamish elbowed him in the stomach.

He wasn't crying.

Maybe a stray tear.

Walking beside her brother, Shanti had made herself a bouquet out of gold measuring spoons with a navy ribbon wrapped around them. Hamish smiled through his non-existent tears at the gesture. She'd respected his distaste for flowers even with her own outfit.

They met in the middle of the circle of their friends. Hamish grasped Akash's hand, tugging him closer. They turned identical glares on Nye when he bungled their names on purpose.

Despite the inauspicious beginning, Nye managed his officiating duties smoothly. Hamish barely recalled any of the words coming out of any of their mouths. He remembered the kiss at the end.

He'd remember it for the rest of his life.

I do.

Those words Hamish would tattoo on his heart until the end of his days. One simple phrase. It signified a vast depth of emotions that he believed he might never be able to adequately express. He'd tried, though, if only for Akash's sake.

As they walked through the honour guard of his work family, Hamish gripped Akash's hand tightly. He offered a handkerchief from his pocket to his husband, who was overwrought by emotion. They dodged through a shower of confetti in the Royal Marine colours of blue, gold, green, and red.

Any thought of skiving off died when Padma cornered the two of them by the stairs. She kissed both of them before lecturing them on not leaving before the toasts, and guided them toward the staircase to the reception.

They could still duck out later for alone time.

Hamish planned on it. He wanted alone time with his husband. *My Akash.* His husband looked absolutely stunning in navy blue silk; he couldn't help wondering if anyone would notice if they disappeared into the loo for an extended period.

Neither he nor Akash was prone to gifts as a way of expressing their affections. They'd talked a number of times about the tradition of grooms exchanging presents. In their eyes, a better option would be to splurge on an epic honeymoon adventure.

As their resident travel expert, Graham suggested Kandolhu in the Maldives. He'd gone once to the island hotel. They planned on staying for two weeks; Hamish intended to ensure Akash was naked for the duration.

It shouldn't be hard, but I will be.

All right, focus. Food, dancing, stupid speeches, and then you can fuck your husband.

In the area usually reserved for dancing, Shanti had again worked her magic. Bolts of navy blue and gold sari fabric had been draped from the ceiling to the walls, cascading gracefully over long tables draped in a similar fabric. Each table setting was perfect and understated. *No flowers.* The table centrepieces were vases etched once again with his company badge, and filled with the same bundles of baking equipment she'd held as her bouquet.

Their fabulous meal of British-Indian fusion had been prepared by Akash's parents and eldest sister. It was served by the bar staff. Hamish drew his husband into an embrace to let him hide his tears at the effort his entire family had gone to for their wedding.

Hamish ignored the whistles around them, and tilted Akash's head up for a more satisfying kiss than the one after the ceremony. "Congratulations, Mr Robinson-Ross."

"Maybe we should've considered our initials becoming R and R." Akash smiled against his lips. "Let's eat. The sooner this is done, the sooner I can get you out of the suit."

The meal smelled and tasted amazing. Hamish had no idea what he'd eaten or how much. Akash distracted him with a hand slipped under the tablecloth to rest directly on his cock.

How the hell am I supposed to have a conversation with people?

Punishment.

There will be punishment.

Toasts were made. Dances were danced. They both danced with Akash's mother and sisters, who made sure to threaten Hamish with bodily harm if they hurt him.

They were sweet and terrifying.

As more and more joined in the dancing, Hamish saw

his chance to grab Akash and run for it. They edged around everyone, ducking out of the building after a whispered goodbye to Akash's parents, who gave them a knowing smile. They tripped up the stairs, laughing and holding hands.

"Akash?"

His husband paused by the exit when Alex caught their attention. "Where've you two been?"

Alice nudged her brother in the shoulder to push him closer. "We stood guard over your Mercedes."

What?

Hamish glanced at Akash, who was equally confused. "Why?"

Alex shoved his hands into his pockets, and his eyes darted around uneasily. "People play pranks at weddings."

"Yes, pranks." Alice nodded sharply. "Don't like pranks."

"We told them off." Alex sounded rather surprised at his own behaviour. "Told them to go away."

"Happy wedding day." Alice dashed forward to hug both of them, then disappeared with her brother.

"What?" Hamish scratched his head, not entirely certain what had happened.

"I believe their wedding present was ensuring no one marked up your vehicle." Akash followed him out of the club toward the car park. "It's sweet. They braved conversation with what I imagine were rowdy former rugby players and soldiers."

"We'll make sure Aled rewards them for us." Hamish looped his arm around Akash to drag him into his arms. "Think your sister will mind if your fancy wedding clothes get wrinkled and ripped?"

"We're not screwing in the car park outside of the club, with CCTV cameras, and everyone that we know within shouting distance." Akash fell into his arms anyway. "What time's our flight?"

"Four hours." Hamish glanced at his watch. "In twenty-three hours, we'll be at our very own villa in the middle of the ocean for two whole weeks."

"Naked."

"You will definitely be naked." Hamish grabbed him firmly by the arse, pushing him against his body. "Let's go get our luggage at your flat."

For the duration of their honeymoon, Ganesh would be staying with Shanti. Hamish got the distinct feeling Akash would be fighting with his sister to get the cat back. A worry for after their honeymoon.

After multiple transfers from plane to plane to seaplane, they finally arrived at the Kandolhu resort to find a certain group of former rugby players had decided to surprise them with an upgrade. They went from a standard beach room to one of the ocean villas with a private pool. Hamish already had images flashing through his mind of them enjoying that perk in particular.

Though tired from their day of travel, Hamish found the warm afternoon sun impossible to resist. They kicked off their travel clothes, dug out swim trunks from their luggage, and dove into the pool. It was pleasantly mild, and they floated around, bumping into each other and enjoying the blissful silence only broken by the waves.

They'd been lucky enough for their new home of two weeks to be at the far end of the semicircle of villas. The one directly next to theirs stood empty, offering them a feeling of complete privacy. Hamish washed off the day of travel in the pool and sun.

As the sun started to dip lower in the sky, Hamish crossed over to where Akash floated on his back with his head and neck resting on the edge of the steps leading into the pool. He'd waited two days for his husband. *All mine.* His patience was not infinite, and had definitely reached its limit.

"I've a distinct feeling you're about to be naughty." Akash watched him through half-open eyes. "We've got maybe an hour before they bring our dinner out to us. I'd rather not give them a show."

Hamish found the hem of Akash's shorts, yanking them off and throwing them up on the deck. "Perhaps a preview of the show for a party of one?"

Not waiting for a response, Hamish lifted Akash out of the water to sit on the edge. Sex in the water would've been romantic, but he had a friend who'd wound up with an infection after engaging in extracurricular activities in a pool. He'd no intentions of ending their honeymoon early for a trip to the hospital.

"Want to hop in the shower to rinse off?" Akash got to his feet before Hamish could act on his original plans.

He watched his husband stride confidently across the deck into their villa, visible through the floor-to-ceiling glass panels. "Get out of the pool, you idiotic arse."

It started in the shower, but they tumbled out of it, dripping water everywhere, stumbling toward the bed with their mouths glued together. Hamish caught Akash before he could trip over one of their bags that had been left in the middle of the floor. They collapsed on the mattress with their limbs tangled, teeth clashing together because neither had wanted the kiss to end.

Eventually separating their lips to catch their breath, Hamish flipped Akash over on his stomach, shoving him into the mattress. He slid down his husband's body, tongue tasting a path down his back to bite him firmly on the arse. His hands gripped each cheek firmly to squeeze roughly.

He pried Akash's cheeks apart, dragging his thumb along the crease. He swirled his finger around before dipping into him. Exploring the golden, toned body at his mercy would always be a highlight of life for Hamish.

His tongue replaced his thumb. Hamish grinned wolfishly at the immediate reaction from Akash. He stroked his shaft lazily to add to the stimulation.

"You're killing me." Akash groaned, his fingers digging into the sheets, bunching them in his hands. "*Hamish.*"

"Don't worry." Hamish manhandled him into a better position. "I'm first aid certified."

"*Arse.*"

"Yours is rather spectacular." He swatted it to prove his point. "Ready for me?"

"Don't tease me. Not now."

With Akash on his side, Hamish pushed his leg up with another quick squeeze to his behind. He teased Akash with the head of his cock briefly, before sinking into him with a hard and satisfying thrust. His lips covered his husband's, muffling their grunts while he drove up into the magnificent heat he found so incredibly addictive.

Akash brought an arm up around Hamish's neck to gain some leverage. He met his thrusts as best he could while reaching down to stroke his own erection. "Fuck. I love you."

"Good," Hamish grunted against his lips. "We have gone and gotten married."

His nose pressed against the side of Akash's head. He breathed in deeply before ramping up his movements. His bollocks slapped against him while he hammered into the man he intended to spend the rest of his life with.

They peaked within seconds of one another. Hamish exploded first. He quickly reached down to wrap his hand around Akash's to speed up his stroking, until he surrendered to the little death as well.

"Shower to clean up before dinner?" Hamish couldn't bring himself to move just yet, and used his arm to prop his body up to avoid crushing Akash. "We wouldn't want to shock them."

"I've a better idea." Akash rolled away from him, hopped off the bed, and strode confidently out the open doors to the steps leading to the clear ocean waters to dive in. "Oh, it's lovely out here."

Saying "so are you" seemed a bit trite. Hamish opted to join him in the warm water instead. They stayed close to the wooden steps, not confident enough to venture far without something covering their bodies. Heaven, he decided, was watching his Aki circle around him in the gentle waves.

Akash nudged by him toward the steps. "I'll grab towels and dry shorts for us both."

Hamish's eyes followed the perfect naked form all the way out of sight into the villa. "Oh, you're so pathetically lost you're never coming back from it."

Supper consisted of steak frites for Hamish and a Maldivian curry for Akash. Ever the baker, his husband wanted to test out new flavours and spices on their honeymoon. They shared a dessert of tiramisu.

Attempted to share a dessert of tiramisu, as Hamish decided midway through it would taste far better eaten off Akash's chest. *And I was right.* They'd christened the deck afterwards and learned an important lesson.

Rough sex on wooden planks hurts—and not in a fun way.

The following morning they headed out on a private charter to sail around for a few hours. They snorkelled for a bit before enjoying a picnic lunch on a deserted island by themselves. Hamish ended up with a sunburn, and Akash had an allergic reaction to something on the island. They returned happily to the villa to collapse on the cushioned deckchairs in the shade.

"Scale of one to ten."

Hamish brought himself out of his doze to blink at Akash. "Scale of one to ten what?"

"How happy are you?"

Hamish threw his arm out to grab the arm of Akash's lounger, and dragged it across the deck until it rested next to his. "Definitely a ten. You?"

"The proof is in the eating, so I suppose we'll see." Akash laughed when Hamish yanked him out of his chair into his own. He straddled his lap. "Thought you'd gotten all sunburnt and intended to never move again?"

"I'm made of sterner stuff." Hamish wrapped his arms tightly around his husband, forcing him to lie squashed up with him in the deckchair. "Stop wiggling around, I'm taking a nap."

"A nap?"

"I'll require my strength to see how many walls in the villa I can fuck you against. I'm partial to the glass ones." Hamish stroked his fingers up Akash's spine until he could thread them into the man's wind whipped hair. "Is this happily ever after, then?"

"Sunburnt in a villa in the Maldives?" Akash rested his chin on Hamish's chest. "No, we're in the proving drawer—the best bits are still to come."

No, the best bit is here in my arms, and I'm never letting him go.

THE END

ACKNOWLEDGMENTS

A massive thank you to my betas, Becky, Olivia and all the brilliant people at Hot Tree, and my beloved hubby who never complains when I'm cursing at my computer.

Thanks to Beardo for sharing his personal experience with how members of the military write letters for loved ones in case they don't make it home. Thank you for your service, and I hope you always find your way safely to your family.

Thanks to all of my readers, whether this is the first or fourth of my stories that you've read. I'm so glad you enjoy the crazy lives of the lads of The Sin Bin as much as I do.

ABOUT THE AUTHOR

Dahlia Donovan wrote her first romance series after a crazy dream about shifters and damsels in distress. She prefers irreverent humour and unconventional characters.

An autistic and occasional hermit, her life wouldn't be complete without her husband and her massive collection of books and video games.

Stay connected with Dahlia:

FACEBOOK: WWW.FACEBOOK.COM/DAHLIADONOVAN

WEBSITE: HTTP://DAHLIADONOVAN.COM

TWITTER: HTTPS://TWITTER.COM/DAHLIADONOVAN

If you enjoyed reading this book, please consider leaving a review.

ABOUT THE PUBLISHER

Hot Tree Publishing opened its doors in 2015 with an aspiration to bring quality fiction to the world of readers. With the initial focus on romance and a wide spread of romance sub-genres, we envision opening to alternative genres in the near future.

Firmly seated in the industry as a leading editing provider to independent authors and small publishing houses, Hot Tree Publishing is the sister company to Hot Tree Editing, founded in 2012. Having established in-house editing and promotions, plus having a well-respected market presence, Hot Tree Publishing endeavours to be a leader in bringing quality stories to the world of readers.

Interested in discovering more amazing reads brought to you by Hot Tree Publishing or perhaps you're interested in submitting a manuscript and joining the HTPubs family? Either way, head over to the website for information:

WWW.HOTTREEPUBLISHING.COM

www.ingramcontent.com/pod-product-compliance
Lightning Source LLC
Chambersburg PA
CBHW050510190726
48284CB00003B/756